T0157316

THE FALL OF
SAINTS

THE FALL OF
SAINTS

A Novel

WANJIKŨ WA NGŨGĨ

ATRIA PAPERBACK

New York   London   Toronto   Sydney   New Delhi

ATRIA PAPERBACK

A Division of Simon & Schuster, Inc.
1230 Avenue of the Americas
New York, NY 10020

First Atria Paperback edition February 2015

ATRIA PAPERBACK and colophon are trademarks of Simon & Schuster, Inc.

For information about special discounts for bulk purchases, please contact Simon & Schuster Special Sales at 1-866-506-1949 or business@simonandschuster.com.

The Simon & Schuster Speakers Bureau can bring authors to your live event. For more information or to book an event, contact the Simon & Schuster Speakers Bureau at 1-866-248-3049 or visit our website at www.simonspeakers.com.

Designed by Rory Panagotopulos

Manufactured in the United States of America

10 9 8 7 6 5 4 3 2 1

The Library of Congress has cataloged the hardcover edition as follows:
Ngūgī wa, Wanjikū.
    The fall of saints : a novel / Wanjikū wa Ngūgī. First Atria hardcover edition.
       pages cm
    1. Husband and wife—Fiction. 2. Secrets—Fiction. 3. Adopted children—Fiction. 4. Families—Fiction. 5. Kenya—Politics and government—Fiction. I. Title.
    PH356.N48F35 2014
    894'.54134—dc23   2013044335

ISBN 978-1-4767-1491-2
ISBN 978-1-4767-6033-9 (pbk)
ISBN 978-1-4767-1493-6 (ebook)

For my daughter, Nyambura Sade Sallinen,
my father, Ngũgĩ wa Thiong'o,

and

To the memory of my late mother,
Minneh Nyambura Ngũgĩ

Part One

1

My cell phone rang. I assumed it was from Detective Ben Underwood again. I looked at the backseat, where my son, Kobi, excitedly cradled his soccer ball; he had scored the winning goal for his side. I answered the phone and asked, "Hey, got more details?"

I heard muffled noise followed by shallow breathing. I took the phone from my ear and checked the caller ID. PRIVATE, it read. It was not Ben.

"Hello . . . Hello?"

No answer. I hung up. It rang again. The same muffled noise.

"What do you want?" I asked, irritated, thinking it was a telemarketer.

"Take this from a friend," said a deep voice in a put-on Jamaican accent. "You ask too many questions."

"Who are you?"

"Just stop it." And the line went dead.

I looked around the car in panic. I instinctively reached out to Kobi, to reassure him, but more myself. He had been through enough in his journey into our lives. But of course only I heard the threat. My hands were shaking. Compose yourself, Mugure. There is nothing to this. A crank call.

I dialed Ben and went over every detail of what had just taken place.

"Are you sure?" he asked.

I felt irritated by his question. "Think I'm making it up?"

"No, no," Ben protested, and told me to let him know if the person called again. "But, Mugure, be careful," he said before he hung up.

I was relieved when Kobi and I found Zack at home. Everything appeared normal again. But I sensed something had come undone.

I first met my husband, Zack, at the office of Okigbo & Okigbo, a law firm in Manhattan, on Canal Street, not far from south Broadway. Actually, the firm was not a partnership, but the double-barreled title made the sole proprietorship appear bigger and more powerful. I was coming from the bathroom back to the reception desk when I literally walked into Zack. His papers went flying all over the corridor.

"Body screening?" he said as I quickly ran about, collecting the papers.

I brought them back, trying to align them, and came face-to-face with a tall, preppy, but strikingly good-looking blond man. He almost let the papers fall again as he frowned and gave me a long hard look. Disapproval, I thought.

"I am really sorry, sir," I managed with a sheepish smile.

"I should sue you for invading my privacy," he said. In what seemed a quick afterthought, he added, "But a cup of coffee would make me forget this ever happened."

"Sounds like a plan," I said without thinking, but then I would have said anything to end the embarrassment.

He had come to meet with my boss for a deposition in a case of medical malpractice. I pointed in the direction of Mr. Okigbo's office. He didn't budge. He continued standing there, as if studying me.

"Umm . . . your number," he said at last.

"Oh, yes, of course, one second, sir. If you can come this way, please," I said, leading him toward Okigbo's office, fumbling in my bag for a card, anything to get him away.

"Mugure. Office manager," he said, glancing at the card.

I hoped he was not being sarcastic about the pretentious title. I was a part-time receptionist and a glorified all-purpose messenger. To complete "all-purpose" for the same wages, Okigbo wanted to have me trained as an armed security guard and even had me go to a shooting range. When my eyes closed and my hands trembled involuntarily at the sight of a gun, my would-be trainer returned a verdict of hopeless that ended whatever security ambitions Okigbo had in store for me.

"Zack Sivonen," he said, "Edward and Palmer Advocates," which was unnecessary because the name and its location, in lower Manhattan, were on the card he gave me. He entered Mr. Okigbo's office. I noticed that he walked with a slight limp, but it suited him, as if it were a style he had cultivated.

On our first date, Zack took me to Shamrock, a club in the basement of a sex shop on Forty-Second Street between Sixth and Eighth Avenues, the red-light district of New York City. Blue fluorescent bulbs lit our descent into a dungeon. Even when the lighting changed into a clearer soft yellow, the atmosphere remained eerie, as in a horror film. The ambient smoke made me cough.

"It gets better, I promise," Zack said, noting my discomfort.

"I sure hope so," I said.

I began to make out the outlines of things. One section of the wall was decorated with colorful stained glass, to give the illusion of windows. The ceiling had been fitted with wooden beams, matching the wooden chairs, which were covered with large pillows. The decor and the seating made it look like more of an old church than a bar.

We chose a table directly in front of a small stage on which the band was assembling instruments. Judging by the bosoms protruding from the waitresses' see-through outfits, it was clear what criteria had been used to hire them.

Soon the club was crowded. The air smelt of fermented ale. I felt so uncomfortable, I began to wonder about Zack's judgment and my own.

Minutes later, several shots of tequila had cleared my larynx and forced my lungs to make peace with the smoke. But it was the voice of the tall dark African American woman belting the blues that finally made me forget the place was a danger to my health. Each note vibrated from her belly. She sang as if every word and gesture and hip motion mattered. Her voice took me on a journey to worlds of rainbow colors. Observing my fascination, Zack asked if I would like to meet her. "Really, you can make it happen?" I blurted.

After the performance, he took me to into a small bar backstage. We found the singer on a barstool, swiveling back and forth as she sipped mineral water from a bottle. She had changed from the stage maxidress into a white cotton shirt over skintight blue jeans tucked into knee-high platform boots.

"Melinda," she said as she stretched out her long hand to greet me.

Up close, under neutral lighting, and without stage makeup, her big eyes and high cheekbones stood out. Her long straightened hair was still combed back, slightly covering her ears, from which hung her trademark, dangling gold earrings. Her dark skin looked smooth, like velvet, and her wide smile revealed a perfect set of white teeth.

"You are beautiful," I said. "With a golden voice."

"You are beautiful, too," she returned the compliment, "but I can't say anything about your voice, because I have not heard you sing."

"Thank you," I said. "I don't have my mother's voice. She was a singer. But she confined it to our local church."

"Really? What a coincidence. My mother sang in church," Melinda said. "I sing in the same choir sometimes."

Just then a tall, broad-shouldered, light-skinned man appeared and growled something. I felt rather than saw Zack tense up.

"Meet Zack's fiancée," Melinda hastened to say, snapping the standoff between the men. "Mugure, this is my husband, Mark. He comes for me every night. Doesn't trust the red lights."

He smiled and shook my hand, nodding to Zack, almost. The change from near hostility to hospitality was fleeting but unmistakable.

We left. Zack let me know that he had dated Melinda

for a few months during their college days at New York University. They had lost contact after graduation but, through sheer coincidence, met up again at Edward and Palmer Advocates, where she did some consulting.

"She's a lawyer?" I said, even more amazed at her many talents.

"No, a financial analyst."

"Who sings in nightclubs and churches?"

"Yes, but don't underestimate her. She's excellent with computers. Call her director of virtual reality," he said, laughing.

"Fascinating," I said. "How does she manage it?"

"With different names. Black Madonna for the club and Black Angel for the choir," he said.

"And as financial analyst?" I asked.

"Meli Virtuoso," he said. "But she plays herself. Melinda."

"And Mark?"

"He's Afro-Mexican but can easily pass for white. Extremely wealthy, humble beginnings, vast landscaping empire. He's established a virtual monopoly in and around the tristate area. We're friends, but he blows hot and cold. He can't get past the fact that Melinda and I once dated. The fiancée thing was meant to reassure him."

Despite the lighting and the smoke, or perhaps because of them and Melinda's voice, Shamrock was addictive, and as Zack and I became lovers, we became regulars. Many people seemed to know Zack, and we saw quite a few on and off the dance floor.

That's why I didn't see it as odd when, one night, a gentleman in a dark suit bumped against us several times, with Zack deftly avoiding a collision. During the break, the suited gentleman left his partner, followed us to our table, and pulled out a chair. Then he casually took out a small gun from inside his jacket, put it on the table, and covered it with his large palms. Zack put a protective arm around me. I was speechless with terror; my eyes never left the gun.

"Of course you don't know me, lawyer," the man said calmly. "Remember the document, drawn and signed in this place?"

"I don't know what you're talking about," Zack said in a level tone.

"But you do! I bring a message from the priest. He has been checking his bank accounts. No deposits lately. It will be a different message next time," he finished, and without waiting for a response, he put the gun back in his jacket and vanished. It happened so quickly that for a second I thought he was an illusion.

"They don't leave me alone. Sometimes they even follow me to the bathroom," Zack said in a steady voice. "It's the notoriety that comes with working for a prominent law firm."

I was surprised by how calmly Zack had taken the incident, but it reassured me to hear him explain. A legal firm was like a church, prison, or hospital. You meet all sorts, they know you, you don't know them, but you act as if you do: It's called public relations. Sometimes they come with a grudge over an issue you have long since forgotten. Attorneys are in the same position as judges. A judge sentences a person and thinks that's the end. The next time, a year, many years later, the criminal faces him with a knife or gun in a crowded marketplace or in a church. "You remember me?" the criminal asks. Of course the judge does not.

"The fact is, I have no clue what the man was about. Crazy. Or a case of mistaken identity. Forget it."

Years later, scrambling for my life in the underbelly of the streets of Nairobi, I would often recall the incident and wonder why I didn't take it as a warning and walk out of Zack's life for good. Instead, the hint of danger and the den's atmosphere of mellowing decadence proved hypnotic.

Besides, Zack came into my life when I most needed a lucky break. I had just earned my first degree from the City College of New York. For a while I tinkered with the idea of going back home to Kenya, but from what my lawyer friend Jane Kagendo told me, Nairobi streets were bustling with unemployed BAs. I stayed on in America, hoping to go to graduate school, though I did not have the money. With my student visa expired, I was caught up in the hide-and-hope-never-to-be-caught existence of an illegal immigrant. It's a life lived underground, accepting any jobs, any wages, lying about one's status even to fellow immigrants, tensing up at a knock on the door or the sight of police officers, always on a nervous edge in bed or on the street.

Although O&O paid me miserably, I stayed with the firm because the owner had promised he would help me get an H1 visa and eventually a green card. The other way to get a green card was to settle down with an American citizen, but my relationships were always short-lived.

The longest and latest was a two-year stint with Sam, a white American, the man from the banks of Ohio, as I used to call him, a commuter relationship sustained via email, Facebook, Internet chats, texting, and occasional sexting, though plagued with uncertainty: We would promise to meet up and talk about our future face-to-face, but whenever we did, we talked about everything else, and only after he had returned to Ohio or I to New York would I remember that we had skirted the issues of marriage and green cards. I broke it off—or, more truthfully, Zack made memories of that relationship fade into a land of it-never-happened. I did not even bother telling Zack about Sam.

Despite our different histories—he with family origins in Estonia, a former Soviet satellite, and I from Kenya, a former British colony—I felt that Zack and I complemented each other. He took control; I let him and felt safe in his certainty. He loved telling and retelling stories drawn from his life; I loved listening and talked little about events in my life.

Once, in a café on lower Broadway with David West, Zack's childhood friend and now colleague at Edward and Palmer, I asked about the limp he carried so well walking or on the dance floor. Zack told a harrowing story of how he'd survived a hit-and-run; his left leg had to be reconstructed with the recovered pieces of his broken bones. David laughed and told a less dramatic version: Zack fell off his motorbike as the two raced each other. Zack was lucky to get away with a fracture and a slightly shorter leg after surgery. I was about to laugh good-humoredly at the different versions when I saw Zack stand up and look at David with cold steely eyes, hissing, "You say I'm lying?" David apologized and mumbled something about memory being unreliable. Zack sat down, smiled at me, and apologized to David for overreacting. Then he laughed, apparently at the absurdity of the situation. We joined the uneasy laughter.

The incident, or rather the steely look, should have given me pause. Instead, I moved into his Manhattan bachelor pad in the winter. In the summer, we moved to a plush home nestled in a cul-de-sac in an affluent neighborhood of Riverdale, on the northwest side of the Bronx. With its tree-lined streets and quaint mansions on gentle slopes, the area combined the best of city and country living. The backyard gave way to a small garden in which I immediately planted herbs and tomatoes. It was here in the garden, on a morning of sunshine with the music of a hummingbird from a nearby hedge, that he knelt and asked me to marry him. I accepted.

We celebrated our wedding, conducted by a justice of the peace in our backyard, with a dinner party for a few friends, among them Melinda, David, Joe, and Mark. The conspicuous absence of my own friends reflected how deeply I had lost contact with the African community abroad, and how unsocial I was in New York. Zack offered to fly in my friend Ciru Mbai, a researcher at Cape Town University in South Africa, but she declined because she was finishing her PhD dissertation. Jane Kagendo, whom I had known since our school days in Msongari, Kenya, accepted Zack's offer of a ticket, but at the last minute she texted to say that she was in the middle of what she called "a weird and complicated case" involving some sort of alternative clinics and could not make it. Zack wondered what I knew of these clinics that would keep my friends away, but I had no clue what Jane was talking about and assured him he would meet her one day.

I brushed off the disappointment. I was too happy to let anything bring me down. The evening started quietly, but as it wore on, and aided by a few drinks, my guests became animated. Their stories revolved around themes of marriage: vows of sickness and health till death do us part, that kind of thing. David told of an inseparable Bronx couple with a nose for the latest gossip about any- and everyone in the Bronx. Though they were husband and wife, they were more like twins.

"But they are twins," Zack interjected, heightening our interest in the ubiquitous couple. He waited for a few seconds, savoring our curiosity. "They are designer twins," he said, explaining that the pair had renewed themselves through cloned body parts grown to their specifications.

This raised cries of no, no, some arguing that despite the 1996 case of Dolly, technology had not reached a level to make a human out of cloned body parts. David, who may have learned not to contradict Zack, said that while it was possible, it seemed to him that the pair had simply taken on each other's personality. "That's what long life can do to a loving couple," he said, looking in the direction of Zack and me.

Not to be outdone, Mark (whose tongue had been loosened by quite a few Jacks on the rocks), let everybody know that he was rich enough to buy immortality. He talked of his success and publicly invited Zack and Joe and everybody else to join him on new business ventures abroad. He was fascinated with Africa and saw many opportunities, he said, looking at me, as if I were somehow a confirmation.

By contrast, Joe, who owned a real estate company in wealthy Fairfield County, Connecticut, did not utter a word about his worth. He believed in man and woman's immortality of joy in bed only, he joked, winking at Zack and me.

Melinda sang my favorite Dusty Springfield song: *The only one who could ever reach me was the son of a preacher man*. Granted, Zack was no preacher's son, but the song was also about finding love in the most unexpected way. It was a special treat for me.

After the song, Mark embraced Melinda and looked around, as if to say, *She's mine*. Joe told her that if she ever got tired of Mark, he would be waiting in the wings, his way of paying a compliment. Joe's incessant flirting and endless compliments, which Melinda accepted with a smile that invited more, may have done it: Mark and Melinda were the first to leave, he literally dragging her away.

Years later, alone in my bed at night, I would go over every word uttered; examine every gesture and facial expression; recall the stories and the laughter, trying to find a piece that would point me to the Lucifer among the angels who celebrated my marriage to Zack that night.

2

I quit my job at O&O, at Zack's suggestion. He was a citizen, so I no longer needed the firm as my path to a green card; I was making peanuts, and he was making tons of money. Besides, we wanted to start a family: I might as well rehearse the life of a stay-at-home wife and mom. I spent my days taking care of Zack: preparing his meals, ironing his clothes, cleaning and tidying a house that needed no cleaning, there being only the two of us, except of course when we had company, but on such occasions we would hire extra help. Bored in the daytime, I looked forward to our evenings in the quest for a baby. We went at it with gusto. Every night. Really, lovemaking is great, but it is greater when pleasure combines with purpose.

Zack often made business trips to Estonia. On those occasions, I didn't find staying at home alone much fun. Zack had set me up with a stash of money in my accounts, and to relieve the boredom, I would immerse myself in visits to Manhattan department stores and shopping malls. After a time, the novelty wore off. During the day, I felt like a Hollywood star, with all the glitz and glamour that comes from money. But at night, enveloped in a strange emptiness, I felt like a piece of wood. Zack once told me that after the collapse of communism and the return of capitalism in Russia, the wives of the nouveaux riches would spend days buying designer outfits and then selling them in flea markets as a way of easing their boredom. At times I felt like one of them but without the courage to dump my stuff on the flea markets of the Bronx and Manhattan. A pattern emerged: In the daytime, the credit card kept me company, and at night, good old gin and tonic. An expanding waistline resulted.

I was irritated to find that, after a few weeks, I could not fit into the clothes I had bought. I joined the All-Purpose Fitness Club in Riverdale, where I worked on my body with yoga, weight lifting, and biking. It was not much excitement. Then I discovered that I could achieve the same ends with the more fun-filled kickboxing. When I grew bored with that, I enrolled in Krav Maga martial arts classes. Krav Maga was not your elegant judo or aikido performance: it was rough and brutal. To my surprise, I found myself warming to the blood rush.

I was never one to keep up with events in Kenya, but now, with a lot of time on my hands, I would browse Kenyan newspapers online, only to be met with the comedy of politicians defecting from one political party to another or a politician forming several political parties. Some moments I thought long and hard about the family I never really knew. I wondered what life must have been like for my mother, pregnant with me in her teen years, banished from home, and forced to cut ties with her siblings. I resented the fact that she seemed insufficiently angry with my absentee father or with fate. For me, coming to America was like an escape from a social void, an absence of feeling that I belonged to a unified family and place. Zack was the nearest I had felt to an identity I had chosen. Nothing could fill his absence when he was in Estonia.

Melinda helped me kill time with stories: a lot about her work as Black Madonna and Black Angel but very little about Meli Virtuoso, the financial analyst. Her work schedule was flexible; she had no problems rearranging it to suit me. We always found things to do together, shopping, mainly. Shamrock was the only place I could not bring myself to go, despite Melinda's constant invitation to be her guest. It was sacred to my union with Zack, and I could never go there without him.

She invited me to her church to hear her sing as Black Angel. She told me that many visitors—the "Jesus is my savior" type—flew all the way from Africa, South Africa, and Kenya to hear the gospel music. There was a Kenyan lady reverend who came to the church in the belief that the choristers were real angels. She insisted on meeting one of them. Melinda offered herself and kept up the illusion that her voice was a direct gift from angels who came to her by night. There are too many crazy reverends, I thought.

Zack had told me that once, in Estonia, he met a Kenyan woman bishop on a mission to convert people from communism. Completely unaware of the fall of the Soviet empire, she had an elaborate moral scheme to smuggle her Christian converts into the West and wanted him to join her.

When Zack resumed his routine between Edward and Palmer during the day and Riverdale at night, we were back on the social circuit and to our nightly quest. And what nights! It was as if each touch whetted our appetite for more. He kissed me, slowly and everywhere, each night working me to new heights from which I would descend into an incredible free fall. Years into our marriage, my stomach still tied itself in knots at the thought of how each night would bring new ways to satisfy our mutual hunger. Tenderness in wildness.

Except that our quests did not bear fruit. Whenever we felt like we had created life, I would buy a self-testing kit, with the same result. A year of fruitless quest took its toll: At night, purpose took over from pleasure. Bedtime increasingly became a time and place of anxiety. The real blow came when a visit to my gynecologist and a battery of tests revealed that, for some reason, I conceived in the tubes, not in the womb, and life would not stay. Childlessness was threatening my marital bliss. I contemplated surrogate motherhood, but Zack was against having another woman carry his seeds. It was me or nobody. It was flattering, though not a solution to my desire to have his baby.

Joe came to the rescue. Among the men who came to the wedding, I liked Joe the best. We hit it off right away. Stocky, medium-sized, with a scar across his face, he loved cigars, women, and fast cars. Zack seemed to rely on him more than he did the others. He was at our place one evening when we poured out our hearts to him. He shrugged off my inability to have babies and suggested adoption. I don't know why we had avoided thinking of this alternative. After Joe left, we continued turning it over, and by the time we nodded off, we had agreed to adopt a child.

Zack suggested Kenya, the land of my birth, as the source, and I was very moved. But would Kenya give us a biracial child? We wanted a baby who reflected our racial identities, and as long as it fulfilled that condition, we did not care where it came from, Africa or America. Through Melinda, Mark suggested the Kasla adoption agency, in Chinatown, claiming that it was known to meet needs such as ours. Zack and I filled out numerous application forms; he handled the whole thing and told me when Kasla had sent a copy of the dossier to the agency's sister company in Kenya. Zack often told me not to judge a book by its cover. For example, Mark's scowling face hid a kind heart.

Zack revived the offer of house help that I had rejected soon after we moved to Riverdale. I hired Rosie, a tall, robust plus-size Ghanaian. I gave her good wages and saved her from having to do three or four jobs. It was not entirely out of charity. I wanted somebody who would be there for me and the baby. It turned out to be a good investment. Rosie entered into the spirit of the moment and supported my hopes. We whiled away the time with gossip and stories. Her own love life was sour: all the good Ghanaian men were taken. Life for her was work in the daytime and loneliness at night. Rosie would never hear of dating someone who was not Ghanaian, least of all a white guy. Love between white men and black women was not true love, she said. "It's more of a mutual curiosity," she claimed, following up the assertion with a loud laugh that moved her chest up and down. "It has worked for me," I countered, "and for me, Zack is more than a curiosity, he is hot." "Well, yes, you are the exception to the rule," she said, "mostly it doesn't work," though she never cited a personal experience.

In no time Rosie became the sibling I did not have in Kenya. I told her how I came to America, an eighteen-year-old who had never left her Ndenderu home in Nairobi, and entered Worcester State University in Massachusetts, where an African was indeed a curiosity. On my first walk outside the campus, I ran to the first black person I saw in the streets who told me that New York was more multicultural. I was not disappointed: At City College, I didn't have to answer questions about a country called Africa, or explain that I had not played with elephants as a child or that we did not live in trees. Rosie had encountered similar questions, even in New York. Our stories of survival, working several jobs here and there, dreams of having an extra dollar to buy ourselves a tiny luxury, were similar, the difference being that I had landed a wealthy husband.

Lost in our life stories, Rosie and I must have scrubbed every corner of the house twice or three times over.

One evening, almost a year since we had started the process, a social worker delivered a beautiful two-year-old boy to our door. I would have preferred to fetch him but Zack had assured me this was okay too. My eyes were so glued to him that I hardly noticed the messenger; I left it to Zack to deal with her.

He had big round adoring eyes, and I loved him the minute I saw him. His brown skin was a fine balance between white and black. The paperwork said little about his background. His parents were not known; he had been left at a church entrance and taken to the police and then the agency. Judging from his given name—Kobi Yusuf—he could have been born in Garissa or, more likely, Mombasa. American navy soldiers had been training there for years. We toyed with giving him a name from both sides of the family.

Zack's family history, like mine, was complicated. His grandmother was estranged from his grandfather. She brought up Eha, Zack's father, single-handedly. Holding

Eha, then seven, she had hidden in the forests to avoid the fate of the tens of thousands of Estonians hurled into railroad cars and deported to Siberia or Kazakhstan during the Soviet occupation. Mother and son escaped in a small boat to Germany and finally to the USA, among the early Estonian immigrants.

Eha grew up in the Bronx and later married Edna, an Italian American schoolteacher. A year later, Zack was born to an absentminded father who spent his days mulling over the fate of his own father, whom he never met. Eha spent entire summers traveling in the US and Russia, diving into archives and libraries, examining this and that record, and asking questions. Failure only whetted his desire to know: Searching for his family became an obsession that intensified with years. In search of his lost family, he neglected the living family.

Then Eha stopped his quest and never mentioned his father's name again. He took to the bottle as if hiding from himself or from whatever he had encountered in his final visit to his homeland. Eha died six months after Edna succumbed to breast cancer. Despite his disgust with his father, Zack may have inherited Eha's obsession to dig up the truth of his past. He told me that although he always went back to Estonia for business, he also wanted to know more about his grandfather. He never forgave his father enough to want to name a baby after him.

My relationship with my father was one of equal absence. My mother, who raised me, was always vague about him, how or where he lived, so I took it that he had abandoned me. I met him only once, in his office, when I turned eighteen, right before I left for the US, and there was no time to unravel the mystery. Why should I reward him by naming my son after him? In the end, we decided to keep Kobi and turned Yusuf into Joseph, in honor of Joe.

Kobi seemed unfazed by the new environment, as if used to sudden changes. I wondered about all the hardships he had gone through that I would never know. Though it would have been good to know his family past for medical purposes, the absence of known facts was a blessing. I could own him completely. His history would be the one we would give him.

You should have seen Zack and me claiming that he already looked like one of us, till Rose laughed and said that he would soon acquire both our features.

"Haven't you seen how spouses in time acquire each other's looks? It is the same with children," Rose said, an observation that reminded me of David's story about the twins.

I gave a party to introduce Kobi to Joe, Mark, and Melinda, thanking them all for the role they had played in the adoption process. Mark protested that he had done nothing to deserve the gratitude, but Melinda stopped the game spoiler with a kiss, saying they were always with us in flesh and spirit. Really, Mark did not know how to let others appreciate his generosity, only his ferocity.

Kobi was somewhat aloof at the start, but I had expected this. I knew I would win his trust and his love. I wanted to be a good mother to this child, as my mother had been to me, and I could see that Zack was equally committed. Kobi took over my life. I hardly noticed Zack's absences.

Though he still traveled, whenever he was home, Zack spent a lot of time with the boy. I enjoyed watching them play soccer or football in the yard. Sometimes they were too engrossed in Frisbee and flying kites to notice me. Melinda joined me a few times and insisted that Kobi had an uncanny resemblance to Zack. "Good," I said. Rosie's observation was confirmed when, on another occasion, Joe found me playing with Kobi and said that he bore an uncanny resemblance to me.

Everything I had made me grateful to Zack. Yesterday I was an illegal immigrant. My mother was dead. My father had denied me. My womb would not carry a life. Zack had given me a home, a country, and a child. In return, I inwardly assured him of my devotion. I made sure he had the privacy he needed and kept Kobi away from his office down the hall from the kitchen. It was the least I could do.

A few years later, with the blood and tears of agony flowing all around me, hope and deliverance precariously resting in the Kenyan police force, I would wonder whether it wasn't a higher order that made me break my pact with myself to stay away from Zack's office.

3

Actually, a rat gave me a reason to finally enter the office. Even before Kobi came into our lives, Zack kept his office locked. I had never needed to enter: I always saw it as the space he needed for himself. After all, I had my little space—which I hardly ever used or locked—and we had an office where we kept papers of common interest. But the little unwelcome guest broke my routine. For a whole week, the creature played tricks, entering at times and in places of its choosing. Sometimes Rosie and Kobi would join me in the chase without success. So I called the exterminators.

Zack and Kobi were out for a drive. The office, which I had left till last, was immaculate. Everything was in its place. A rat would never find something to eat or a corner to hide. I had it fumigated all the same. After writing the exterminator a check, I went back to the office to ensure that everything was back in place. A piece of paper stuck out of a file in one of the drawers. I pulled the file with the intention of retrieving the paper, but instead, the entire folder landed on the floor. And with it, a gun.

I held the thing in my hands briefly: It brought back

memories of my brief moment at the shooting range and the encounter with the gunman at Shamrock. Zack obviously had the same love affair with guns as all Americans. I was afraid of guns and quickly put it back in the drawer. More worrisome were the scattered papers, reminiscent of my first encounter with Zack. He might well think I did these things on purpose.

I started to assemble them. As I did, I saw Kobi's name and a phone number on a piece of paper. I shoved the scrap in my pocket and put the folder back in place. Flustered, I closed the door and went downstairs, and retrieved the piece of paper from my pocket. Besides Kobi's name and a phone number, there was nothing else on the piece of paper. I paused. The number did not ring a bell. I flipped the piece of paper. Nothing on the back. What had the number to do with my son? Was it the adoption agency's? Or . . . could it belong to another woman? Curiosity aroused, I picked up the phone, not sure what I would say. Then I put it down. Better to use my cell phone. The number I dialed was currently not available, said the answering robot.

"What is wrong with me?" I muttered to myself. Zack could have been talking about Kobi and scribbled down his name in the process. I felt bad for suspecting Zack of secret telephone liaisons with another woman. He had never given me reason; he had been very open about his affairs before we married, including his stint with Melinda. I had kept my relationship with the man from Ohio to myself. Zack and Melinda had maintained a healthy relationship of mutual respect and friendship. I had erased mine with Sam, not even opening his emails.

Boisterous noise downstairs alerted me that Zack and Kobi had returned. I put the paper in my side drawer, tucked under some other stuff, and went downstairs, a little flustered at my furtive behavior.

"Hi, Mommy, did they find the rat?" Kobi asked when I joined them in the kitchen.

"No, they didn't but the poison will get him."

The next day, after I dropped Kobi off at school, I went upstairs, took out the piece of paper, and scrutinized it. I saw some faint writing on the back. I held it against the light, then walked to the window, squinting really hard.

What in the world was Alaska E-S? Zack had never talked about Alaska except in connection with Sarah Palin. I went downstairs and pulled out the directory. There were hundreds of businesses named Alaska. I looked at the paper again, determined to figure out what the other letters were. I could not make them out. Convincing myself that I was seeing a mountain where there was a molehill, I tore up the piece of paper and threw it into the incinerator. I laughed at my paranoia. So absurd. I put the incident out of my mind and resumed my family and social life, which amounted to a party now and then.

One lazy Sunday, I woke up, my head pounding as if someone were inside it playing drums. Zack and I had drunk more than our fair share of alcohol at a party the previous night. I'd hoped that father and son could go to the soccer game without me, but a quick glance at Zack sprawled dead asleep on the bed told me I'd be going with Kobi, without Zack. Kobi was very proud of Dad and Mom as witnesses to his heroics. His team, Park Boys FC, was playing against the formidable Little Giants FC at Macombs Dam Park, across from Yankee Stadium. I swallowed a painkiller, drowned it with liters of water, and forced myself to pack some snacks and juice. I dragged myself alongside an excited five-year-old Kobi, strutting about in his cute little blue uniform.

My car would not start. The battery was dead. I must have left the lights on. I rushed upstairs. Zack was still fast asleep. I scribbled a note: *Honey, took your car, mine won't start. Call AAA.*

Kobi had a way with the ball and scored both of the team's goals, not unusual for him. One was a spectacular shot from the top right corner of the field. It earned him a roar from the crowd. We decided to celebrate by treating ourselves to some ice cream.

The little shop at Concourse Village East wasn't far from Zack's alma mater, the Alfred E. Smith High School, and Kobi was always happy that we got our ice cream from the same place his father had gone to as a boy. I parked on the street next to the shop. Kobi jumped out to get the ice cream. He loved this little responsibility, as it made him feel grown up. I never let on that I could see exactly what was going on right from the car. He had adjusted well and was growing taller by the day. I felt so proud of him.

Briefly, I turned my gaze from Kobi to the car, and it became clear why Zack liked taking my car when we went out. Mine was always clean. Rosie and I saw to it. The condition of his car was a complete contrast to that of his office and clothes. A thin carpet of dust covered the dashboard. Torn McDonald's and Burger King wrappers lay scattered on the floor and crammed into the ashtray. No wonder his waist had been getting thicker. And couldn't he at least throw away the napkins? How disgusting, I thought, assuming the thing was soiled with ketchup. I pulled the ashtray, took out the napkin, and stuffed it into a paper cup that had been lying about. I looked at the ashtray again only to see yet another piece of white paper. I tried to remove it, using my index and middle fingers, but it got stuck. I got a hairpin from my handbag and started digging it out from the sides, then pulled again. This time it came out easily. I was about to roll it up when I saw *Alaska Enterprises* and a phone number written on it. Intriguing, I thought. "Enterprises" must be the missing word from the other piece of paper, though the telephone number seemed different. I should have kept a record of the other number.

Kobi was making his way back, balancing the ice cream cups. I had the urge to jump out and assist, but I held back. It would feel so much better for him later, when he narrated how he bought the ice cream by himself and safely brought it to the car. He came around to the driver's side and handed me my cup of ice cream and his to hold as he jumped into the backseat.

"Thank you, little man," I said, handing him his.

"You are welcome, Mommy."

"Now I have to teach you how to drive so you can come out here and get the ice cream," I joked.

"Mooommy," he said, laughing as he took a bite, and I joined him.

My latest discovery revived my suspicions of another woman. The following day, I called the new number. This time a voice answered after two rings. It was male; I had expected a female voice. I was confused and just caught the words "export," "import," and "Africa." I hesitated. I felt really silly and blurted the first words that came to my tongue: Could I speak to Zack Sivonen? They did not have a Zack Sivonen in the office, the voice said.

"Oh, wrong number," I said, and quickly hung up, not even asking their location. I could have kicked myself. Surely I had better things to do, I admonished myself. But *that* was a problem; I didn't have much better to do. Shopping, except for Kobi, no longer excited me. Rosie did the major housecleaning and even cooked sometimes. Zack and I liked Ghanaian dishes. Gari, peanut soup, and meat reminded me of the *ugali* and *sukuma wiki* in Kenya. Kobi liked okra soup and *kenkey*. But deep inside, I knew that even if I had something that kept me busy all day and night, these pieces of paper and telephone numbers still would have troubled me.

The following day I dropped Kobi off at school and went to meet my close friend Melinda.

4

Mark had been the only blemish in my friendship with Melinda. It had nothing to do with his remarkable rise from poverty to wealth. His parents entered the US as contract workers under the notorious Bracero Program, which allowed Mexican cheap labor on American farms. "To do the work mostly scorned by Americans," Mark liked to say. His parents had stayed after the program ended, but they remained trapped in a cycle of poverty from which Mark had been able to break free. His was a story to admire, but his grumpy attitude when we first met at Shamrock and later, at the wedding, had put me off. And yet he had a compassionate and modest side: He had helped us in our search for a baby and would not publicly brag about his role in our happiness.

This attractive side did not square with his treatment of Melinda. I didn't understand the causes of their constant friction, but when she came to our place distraught one day, she and I had a heart-to-heart. Though Zack was home, she and I managed some private time.

"Jealousy," she said, responding to my concern. "He

dislikes my singing in nightclubs. He wants me to quit Shamrock and stick to the church choir. He says he has enough money to maintain me the way Zack keeps you. But I don't want to be a kept woman," she said, holding back tears. "He says I am bad and wants to straighten me out with love. Am I really that bad, Mugure?"

"Of course not. He is a male chauvinist and wants to suppress your talent." I said, not too pleased that he saw me as the ideal of a kept woman.

I offered her a room to rest. When Mark's car pulled up the driveway a couple of hours later, I went out to confront him. "Mark! Beating your wife senseless seems to be your special skill, eh?" I said to him as he got out of the car.

"Good morning to you, too," he said, ignoring my confrontation.

"One of these days you are going to kill her."

"Don't get dramatic now. No one is going to die," he said.

"You should just leave her if you can't deal with the attention she gets."

"I see she has gotten to you, too," he said as he walked up to the house with casual indifference. "You know her voice but not the person behind the voice. I do. And do you know what? I love her. That's my only problem."

An hour later, Melinda and Mark came downstairs hand in hand. "She just exhibited battered woman's syndrome," I told Zack after they were gone. "Melinda is an adult and should be left alone to make her choices and decisions," was all he said.

One day she called me from the Holiday Inn in SoHo with the good news that she had finally left Mark. I drove there and accompanied her to the law offices of Jameson Batts, two blocks away. She could have engaged Edward and Palmer, she told me, but Zack and Mark's male bonding might create a conflict of interests. Mark was not pleased with my role in the divorce. A day later, he stopped at my place, wagged a finger at me, and hissed, "You will pay for this," then left.

Months later, in Kenya, I would recall his words and ask myself why on earth I did not take them seriously. If only I had . . . But hindsight is twenty-twenty. At the moment of their utterance, I took them to mean no more than the frustration of thwarted love, and I soon forgot about the warning. I did not even bother to tell Zack or Melinda about it. That weekend Zack and I went to hear her at Shamrock, and she had everybody on their feet as she sang: *I am a free woman* . . .

With Mark out of the way, my friendship with Melinda flourished. She traveled abroad as Black Madonna, performing in major cities. At home, she juggled her time among nightclubs, churches, and financial houses. Her work schedule was flexible, and she often changed it to spend time with me. I came to rely on her.

Today Melinda and I had planned a get-together at our favorite place, Classic Café, on West Fourth Street, near Washington Square Park. I don't know why I bothered to bring a car into Manhattan. It was always so crowded, and the honking from the yellow cabs could easily give one an attack of road rage. I had more time than regular workingmen and -women, so my struggle with the traffic was another way of whiling away the day.

I left my car at the valet parking lot on Broadway. Waverly Place bustled with students from Zack's alma mater, New York University. Washington Square Park had its usual carnival air. A man sat on a bench, pigeons on his arms, shoulder, and head. Another man in a dark blue suit was muttering, "I will be back, I will be back," furious with himself for having lost a chess game to a homeless man. A white man in dreadlocks started walking alongside me, offering me a joint, telling me he was an artist specializing in pictures of Bob Marley. At the marble arch, he stopped and accosted another passerby. In a few hundred feet, I was at the Classic Café.

"Hey, girl, I see you are still wearing your graduate suit," I said to Melinda, who was dressed, as always, in a skirt suit. I preferred her in maxidresses, but she wore them for performances only.

She made as if to punch me and laughed out loud at the same time. The happy carefree woman had taken over from the battered woman. But today I had not come for social chitchat only. I dug in my bag. She picked up the piece of paper and read it out loud: "Alaska Enterprises." She stopped, gave me a puzzled look, and then was thoughtful for a while.

"I found it in my husband's car," I hastened to say.

"But do you know this company?" she asked.

"I don't," I answered. "Why?"

Again she looked thoughtful, as if weighing the words she would use. "Has Mark spoken to you, or Zack? Made proposals, that kind of thing?"

"Why?" I asked, feeling under interrogation.

"All the years I was with Mark," she continued, "I was never able to understand how he became a millionaire from landscaping only. Most of his employees are illegal immigrants. I have always wondered if he was involved in smuggling illegals across the Mexican border."

"Really?" I asked, with my eyes wide open.

"I am not quite sure, but trust me. I would be careful. One day Mark's business empire will collapse, the chips will fall, and not where you would want them to fall."

She was so serious, and yet her answer felt vague. I came clean about the recent history, starting with the paper on which Kobi's name was written, hoping to draw out more from her.

"What does Kobi have to do with Alaska?" she asked me. "Are you sure it's not a just a mix-up, that Zack just happened to write the name right next to the company's name?"

Her questions mirrored my earlier reasoning. And by the time she said Zack should keep away from Mark—in matters of business, at least—I had arrived at the same thought. Not that we had established the company existed, but her insistence that I keep Zack away from Mark was the ammunition I needed to confront Zack.

Zack had just arrived when I got home, and I did not wait for him to sit down. "What is this Alaska business?" I asked.

Zack was startled by my abrupt question and for a moment looked confused. "What are you talking about?" he asked.

It was my turn to be confused. I did not want to tell him about the pieces of paper; then I would have to tell him how I came by them. "Alaska cropped up in my conversation with Melinda today."

"Wait a minute, Mugure. What does your conversation with Melinda about Alaska have to do with me?" he asked, shrugging.

"Well, just in case you are working with Mark, Melinda said that Alaska might be Mark's company. Please take this as cautionary. She must know some stuff about Mark that we don't."

"Melinda is still bitter about Mark," Zack said, ignoring my suggestion. "He is many things, but I wouldn't go so far as to say he is a criminal. He may employ illegal immigrants at miserly wages, but many employers do that. Cheap labor. Why not? America was built on the cheapest of labor: free labor," he concluded matter-of-factly, not implying moral censure. "Civilizations are!"

Might Mark have gotten us mixed up in his enterprises without Zack realizing? He was probably protecting Mark, I thought, recalling Melinda's talk of male bonding, but I didn't see why I should have to be part of it. Mark was no longer Melinda's husband: I owed him nothing. Melinda's insinuations and Zack's vagueness generated more questions in my mind. I didn't want any chips of his collapsing business empire to fall anywhere near my family. Besides, I now recalled him wagging his fingers at me. I had to do something about it.

I had never really looked at the adoption papers after signing them. Now I decided to review them. I left Zack at the kitchen table bending over a law journal and went to get Kobi's file from our common office, where I had put it about three years ago. The file was not in its usual place. I asked Zack if he knew where it was.

"Why do you need it?" he asked, barely looking up.

"Oh, the school wants his immunization history," I lied.

We searched for the papers all over the house, Zack in his office, while I did the basement.

"Nothing in the office," Zack said as he joined me upstairs. "Are you sure you didn't remove the file, honey?"

"I can't recall doing it," I said.

"Who at the school called for it?"

"The school nurse," I lied again.

"I can check the information tomorrow. Get copies, I hope."

I felt awful, making Zack run around looking for something that the school didn't really need.

Zack called me from work the next day to tell me that he'd faxed me the details and done the same for the school, attention of the nurse, thus saving me a trip there. "Damn!" I said after hanging up. I couldn't very well tell the school that the information had been sent by mistake. So when the phone rang later and the caller identified herself as the school nurse, I started by apologizing for the mix-up. All the same, she asked to see me.

I was at her office early the next day. She told me she had noted some discrepancies between the information we had provided the school a few years ago and what was faxed yesterday. Curious, I pulled my chair close to the nurse's and peered at the papers spread over the table.

The original papers indicated that Kobi had been immunized at a Mombasa hospital in January; the other said Malindi, in October. The dates of birth also conflicted, the recent fax indicating that he was a year younger. I was puzzled but assumed the confusion originated with the adoption agency.

"One last thing," the nurse said. "I am not sure if this is important, but I thought I should mention it anyway. Here it says his mother's name is Abla, father unknown. In the other, it says parents unknown. It's as if this information is for a completely different child."

I asked the nurse to make me a copy of the information. I could hardly wait for Zack to come home. Before he could set his briefcase down, I was on his case. "Zack, do you realize the information you faxed to the school does not match the papers we originally gave them?"

He stopped in his tracks. He stalled for a minute and then turned to look at me. "Let me see the papers," he said, putting his briefcase down.

I pointed out the discrepancy.

"Oh my, Mugure, what do you think this means?" he asked, looking up at me, equally shocked.

"You should know. Where did you get that information?"

"From the adoption agency, of course. There has to be an explanation."

"I will go there," I told him. "Where's their exact location, anyway?"

"It's close to my office. I will go there first thing in the morning, so please don't worry."

"Could this affect Kobi?" I asked.

Zack rubbed his temples, like he did when he was frustrated. "We did everything by the book, so I don't think we have anything to worry about. It's probably a bureaucratic error," he said at last.

The following afternoon Zack called from his office and astonished me with the news that the agency had closed down.

"What?" I screamed in disbelief.

"No one was picking up the phone, so I drove there. Locked up. No forwarding address. This is crazy."

"But they faxed you the information just the other day?" I said.

"It may mean they have just closed down," said Zack, sounding flustered.

"There has to be a way. We have to find them. We have to get the information," I insisted.

"Mugure, calm down. I am a lawyer, remember—I'll see what I can do."

"See? See what you can do? Just do it. It's Kobi's life," I yelled, surprising myself. I had never raised my voice to him before. The tone did not escape him. He tried to soothe me.

"There's nothing to worry about. We are under no obligation to give any background information as a condition of Kobi's place in the school. We need not concern ourselves with his past. Only with the future."

He was right. The school had not asked for the information. And unknowingly, he'd hit me at a different level. He had echoed my attitude about the past, or rather, my philosophy. I had never concerned myself with my past; I had decided not to let the past hold me back. If I ignored it long enough, it would leave me alone to pursue my future. I suppose that's why I'd never pressed my mother to tell me more about my father or probed into the real what, when, why, and how of my past. Why hadn't he bothered to visit me when I was born, at least? How was it that he hadn't been curious enough to find out about his own kid?

"I need the exact address of Kasla," I demanded in a softer voice.

Zack must have sensed something in my silence, hesitancy, and a change of mood. He dictated it over the phone and then added, "Please don't do anything foolish. I will get to the bottom of this. And please keep this within the family," he emphasized as he hung up the phone.

No, no, honey, I said to myself. A flag has been raised. Something is not adding up. Almost as a defiant reaction to Zack's admonition, I called Melinda and told her everything. She was concerned. Always ready for adventure, she suggested we drive down to Manhattan to visit the adoption agency's old address and confirm the closure for ourselves. We agreed on the next day.

I picked up Melinda at the corner of Park Avenue and Fortieth Street. She was dressed in a blue suit and high heels; she had just concluded a meeting with a client. She hopped in, flung her briefcase in the back of the car, fastened her seat belt, and waved her fist in the air. "I am ready for war," she announced.

"Oh, please," I said, smiling. "The agency was your recommendation, remember?"

"Mark's," she said. "I was merely the conduit of good hope."

Yellow was the dominant color in the ever busy Manhattan traffic, thanks to the ubiquitous cabs whose drivers kept giving me the middle finger, a few even lowering their windows to shout something unflattering about female drivers. In her warrior mood, Melinda would shout back or show them the same finger. I didn't enter the war but continued weaving in and out of the lanes, down Broadway to Chinatown. After circling the block, I got a parking space half a block away from our destination.

The smells of soy sauce and pepper were a cruel reminder to my belly that I had not eaten lunch. Melinda said her tummy agreed with mine, and we entered the very next restaurant. It was crowded with men and women in suits. "Chinatown feeds the business district of New York," Melinda commented. "Do you know," she continued as we tackled our chicken and noodles, trying but not too successfully to use chopsticks, "that New York claims this is the biggest Chinatown outside China?" I said, "I've heard that Los Angeles makes the same claim." "And San Francisco," we said in unison, and laughed.

Our tummies full, we walked on and soon came to the supposed location of Kasla. It was a building with huge padlocks on the metal doors.

"They definitely moved, it's confirmed," Melinda said as we stood outside, staring at and then trying the giant padlocks as if they would somehow open at a call of "open sesame."

My head spun with unanswered questions: the conflicting immunization dates; whether Kobi had nameless parents or a parent named Abla; the links between Kasla, now closed, and the Alaska Enterprises. Melinda's suspicions of Mark, vague though they were, added to the confusion, but the biggest puzzle was that Zack had called them the day before and they had responded by faxing the papers.

"Zack spoke to somebody," I said. "That somebody faxed those papers to Zack. So to whom did he speak? From what location? From what machine?"

"Simple. Ask Zack," Melinda said, but she added a rider: "He probably called, and they faxed him some paper with the hope that he would get off their backs. They may have closed the agency and still exist virtually. You don't need a physical space in these days of the Internet. As a financial analyst, I deal with many companies that exist online."

It was plausible. But something was amiss.

"You're the computer kid. Can you see if this Kasla exists online? Track them down in cyberspace."

"I will see," she said. "I am a specialist in cyber war-fare!"

Melinda was right about one thing. I should ask Zack. Yes, ask Zack. He had talked of visiting a physical place and not some cyberspace. And then the unthinkable crept in.

Then I did not realize that in a few months, in the deadly Kenyan streets, hunted on all sides by forces that were not yet clear to me, I would shudder at the recall of the sudden attack of doubt, the moment of disbelief, the inner fight to cling to the previous state of certainty, the question rearing its head, barring my attempt to return to innocence: Was Zack involved in deceit, and knowingly?

We were on the road. My instinct was to rush back and confront him. I caught myself pressing heavily on the gas pedal. I pulled over to compose myself.

A little panic seized me. "No, I have to get my facts right," I murmured to myself, fighting back the doubt. Panic gave way to confusion: Where and how was I going to get the facts? Then I recalled a possible ally. Ben the African.

5

I was in my fourth year at City College of New York when I first met Ben. It was a Friday, and I was walking alone on Amsterdam Avenue, probably mulling, or wallowing in self-pity, over what to do with myself now that my undergraduate studies were coming to an end. A man blocked my way with the oddest of questions: "Are you celebrating Gologo Festival?"

"What?" I asked, wondering what he was talking about. But for the oddity of the question, its sheer unexpectedness, I probably would have ignored the intruder and moved on. I had encountered too many guys who used all sorts of tricks to initiate a conversation.

"Hey, did you forget our day?" he asked.

"Our day?" I said, thinking that this was a case of mistaken identity.

"The day we dance and pray to ensure plentiful rain and good fortune?" he said, handing me a leaflet. He did not even allow me time to read it. He kept bombarding me with questions and unsolicited advice. "How can you call yourself an African and forget to pay homage to our ancestors? No wonder things in Africa are going wrong. We have lost our way."

I was convinced it was he who had lost it. When I found out that Gologo Festival was indeed celebrated by the Talensi people of Tong-Zug in Ghana, I thought he probably wasn't that crazy.

Later, I met him again, this time on Nicholas Avenue, in a repeat of the first encounter, only this time he walked alongside me. "So I see that you are going to the dance?'

"The dance?" I honestly did not know of such an event. I thought it was his way of trying to pick me up.

"It's organized by black students, you know? African Liberation Day. Established on May twenty-fifth in Addis Ababa. Capital of African history. Hail Haile Selassie, King of Kings, Lion of Judah. Ras Tafari. Ethiopia was never occupied by the West. It speaks of our glory. By the way, my name is Underwood. Ben Underwood, but you can call me—"

I dashed to the right abruptly, mumbling something about going to the library, and left him going on about Ethiopia. "Hey, where are you going?" I heard him say, and I could not help a parting shot: "To dig up the glory of our history!" Was he a student? A scholar? A recent arrival on the campus?

It was weeks before I learned that Ben was a police officer, detective division, and often went undercover. Ben was tall and rough-looking, but he had the bluest eyes I had ever seen. Well, on a black brother. Actually, Ben was not black the way Melinda and I were; he was clearly a product of black and white somewhere in his past. He had been serving in the police force all of his adult life, or rather, he had inherited a family legacy of public service: His father and his grandfather had been police officers.

When he wasn't on duty, he always wore dashiki shirts and a hat, and he often carried a cane. He said it was spiritual. He once asked to see me on an urgent matter. He had something he wanted me to help him identify. He suggested we meet at the café known as Classic. I thought it might have something to do with a criminal investigation, and I felt a momentary sense of power: I, Mugure, a student visa carrier, helping a seasoned New York detective bust a criminal? I had a momentary vision of a gunfight, except that I didn't like guns, but then I saw myself taking cover behind a police vehicle, hoping not to be caught in the cross fire.

"Hey, Mugure, how can I cook this?" he asked, holding a white oval rootlike plant in his hand. We had hardly ordered our coffee.

"Where did you get it?"

"Chinese market."

"A crime scene?" I asked, still in my cross-fire mood.

"No, no, a regular market. They sell all sorts of herbs, alternative medicines."

"What is it?" I asked, taking a closer look, a little disappointed.

"You should know. The seller, an old Chinese man, told me it was an African root. That's why I bought it. Here, hold it, doesn't it ring a bell?"

"Ben," I said after briefly looking at the root and giving it back to him, "this could be from anywhere, really!"

"But it's African! Just tell me how to cook it, and the ingredients . . ."

I had to end this. "Okay. Listen carefully. Boil it, but

don't drink the liquid or eat the root. Go to the nearest tree and pour libation to our ancestors while chanting a sacred song or poem to our ancestors."

"Thank you, Mugure," he said, and started reciting Senghor's "Prayer to Masks."

People in the café had stopped to look at him. I wanted the floor to open and swallow me instantly. "Ben, no, not here. Under a tree with a huge trunk and big roots," I said, tugging at his dashiki.

That's when I started calling him Ben the African.

He read quite a lot and was fun to be with, and I suspected that in his work, he put the comical Ben aside. Or maybe it was his cover. I accepted an occasional coffee date with him. He would not touch alcohol; he had a theory that it was a drug the white man had used to weaken the minds and bodies of Native Americans, Australians, and the Canadian First Nations. "Poison and plunder" was how he put it. White people were behind the drug trafficking aimed at ensnaring black folk.

He was attached to a unit working on the World Trade Center remains after 9/11. Believing there was a conspiracy to hide the number of African, black, and non-Caucasian victims, he spent his free time researching this aspect, using his skills as a historical detective, checking dental remains . . . During these conversations, I would drift away, and when he noticed, he would try to recapture my attention with more dramatic theories.

Sometimes I wished I hadn't told him I came from Kenya—what he called the land of Barack Obama's African ancestors—for whenever I met him, in company or alone, he would talk endlessly about his friend Detective Johnston. Apparently, Ben had been sent on a secret mission to track down some white drug dealers who, disguised as Somalis, used piracy as a cover for their nefarious trade, which somehow reached major American cities. Ben had chased the gang across forests and valleys but had lost them in the north, near the Somali border with Kenya. The less well-known East African drug route was beginning to rival the one through Nigeria, although it had not reached the Mexican border. On the way back, his Land Rover got stuck in the mud, and he found himself encircled by a thousand spears.

Ben regretted that he did not know African—he called all African languages "African"—and so could not talk to his black brothers. The white man's language had come between him and his people, he lamented. He would have died that day if Detective Johnston had not aided him. Johnston was then in a division that worked to keep smugglers from crossing borders and was on a routine patrol. That was how they first met, in the wild, a kind of black Livingstone and Stanley—Ben, I presume?—and then became lifelong friends. I was pretty sure Ben's Johnston was not real, and no spears had ever encircled him, and the chase was a rewrite of a western on an African landscape. It was Ben playing the hero in stereotypical African villages. I expected his fantasy to take him to the next level—killing a lion in hand-to-claw combat—but it never came to that.

I don't know at what point Ben fell in love with me or claimed to do so. At first I thought him merely playful when he talked about my dark skin. I was the dream woman who would supplement the black side of his heritage. "You see, Mugure? Look at my Bob Marley skin and yours. My white great-great-grandfather raped my

black great-great-grandmother. I must marry deep black
to strengthen my black heritage."

I could never offer him anything deeper than friendship and the name Ben the African, for which he seemed
eternally grateful. When he found out that I was dating
white boys, he was really upset, as if I had betrayed him
and my Africanness. At first he thought that I was merely
experimenting and would outgrow the desire, but when I
told him about my relationship with Sam, he became visibly shaken. No matter how hard I tried to convince him,
Ben refused to meet Sam. His love changed into a mission
to rescue me from my white captors and restore me to my
African roots. At times I felt as if he had been sent by my
father, whose farewell words were a call for me to beware
of white boys.

Ben's missionary fervor never wavered, even after my
marriage to Zack. Ben had worked in every precinct in
New York but moved to the Bronx a year or so after my
wedding. I sometimes suspected that he'd befriended Zack
in order to keep an eye on me.

But now, in my hour of need, it meant I didn't have far
to drive, and I was grateful. The precinct seemed empty,
with only a few officers walking about. Ben welcomed me
to sit, his desk between us. A map of Africa hung on his
wall, and little wooden sculptures were positioned across
his desk. His taste in African art was good: The sculptures
were very much alive, not the wood carvings of giraffes
and elephants so beloved by tourists.

"The Kasla agency?" Ben asked after I had told him
the reason for my visit. "Hmmm, well, well. And this is the
agency that assisted you in adopting Kobi, you say?"

"Yes."

"Tell me, Mugure," he asked directly. "Why did you marry Zack?"

"Ben, I came to you for help, not marriage counseling," I said, taken aback.

"Sorry, sister. The question may have come out awkwardly, but how well do you know Zack?'

I kept quiet. What could I tell him? That Zack was born of Estonian parents? That he was obsessed with his grandfather the way his father, Eha, had been? That he frequently made trips to Estonia and Eastern Europe and stayed for days without contact?

"What do you mean?" I asked.

"His background, that kind of thing. Do you know anything about his business dealings in Estonia? Eastern Europe?"

How could I bring myself to pour out my personal feelings to Ben? I had been to Estonia once. On our honeymoon. Via Finland. Zack had told me that a boat ride to Estonia from Helsinki would be a more personal entry into the land of his forefathers. We sat on the deck, I leaning on Zack's shoulder, and as the cruise ship drifted on the Baltic Sea, we watched Helsinki, with its forests and lakes and towers, disappear in the distance. Then it was us, the boat, and the blue waters. The excitement coursing through his body as we disembarked and touched the land of his forefathers became mine. No, no, I was not about to share that with Ben.

Instead, I wanted to tell him about our stay in a hotel by the medieval market in the old part of Tallinn, where I never stopped marveling at the centuries-old buildings; the feel of cobblestone under my shoes; the iron streetlamps that lit up the lanes; and the occasional horse-drawn carriage. We often sat in the sidewalk cafés and watched bridal parties walking by; the huge churches with Gothic spires against the skyline and the flowers all over the courtyards provided a romantic background for wedding photographs.

"But you never actually met any of his family or business associates?" Ben asked, interrupting my thoughts with his eyes still fixed on me.

"Come to think of it, I never did," I said.

"Have you been to his office?"

"Actually, no," I said, and felt even more foolish. "But I know some of his colleagues. David West is Zack's childhood friend."

"Mugure, what exactly are you looking for? What are you hoping to find?"

"Nothing, I hope," I said, laughing sheepishly, trying hard not to appear stupid. I found it difficult to admit that I harbored doubts about my husband. "Just curiosity. Why would an agency shut down after sending Zack a document that contradicts the original?"

I thought Ben would laugh off my question, but he didn't. He continued staring at me, as if waiting for more reasons. To try and gauge what he was thinking, I used an argument closer to his heart. "You always talk about black people knowing our past. Isn't it natural that a mother should want to know her child's past?"

"Yes, but this is different. Listen, sister. If your child is adopted legally and you have no problems with him or anyone, I don't see why you need to look any further. Just let it go."

I was taken aback by the statement; it was an echo of what Zack had told me. "Yes, but I . . . I just . . ." I paused.

"May I ask you another question?"

He was being a little too formal, and yet I didn't want him to be personal. "Ben, you can ask anything."

"Except about your marriage," he said. "Did you handle the transactions yourself?"

"No."

"And the people or person who brought the baby, did you see them?"

"I was too excited to see anyone but the baby. Why?" I asked guardedly.

"Because if you did, you could help me by describing the people you dealt with."

"Zack handled everything."

"If I were you, sister," Ben said after some silence, "I would let sleeping dogs lie. But I will snoop around, look up some files, ask the other officers. If something comes up, I will call you."

He had told me that to mollify me, I said to myself. Still, I was surprised that he had echoed Zack's words. Perhaps I'd better stop shadowboxing with ghosts, I thought.

But I didn't see any harm in making one more trip to the agency.

In under half an hour, I pulled up to the street and parked in a lot across from the padlocked building. For a moment I stood there, confused, wondering if I had come to the wrong street or the wrong address. The shop, padlocked yesterday, was now open. I jumped out of the car and half ran toward it, as if I feared it would close again. I entered.

It was a curio shop. There was no one in sight. I stood there looking at all manner of wood carvings of lions, giraffes, zebras, elephants, rhinos, spear-wielding Maasai, and heavily but colorfully beaded women. They reminded me of the ones I had seen in Ben's office, with the same vitality. Had Ben gotten his from here? Just then I saw the head of a rhino coming toward me from inside the shop. I felt like running out, but curiosity and my mission held me in place. The man playing the rhino removed the mask and stood behind the counter. He was tall, bald, midforties, dressed casually in beige pants and a white shirt, a less frightening figure now.

"These are no ordinary carvings," he said.

Did I detect a Jamaican accent? For some reason, it reminded of the dreadlocked man who had followed me in the park, trying to sell me a joint. Or . . . the voice . . . No, I didn't want to go there. Telephones distorted voices.

"Why?" I asked, to create a friendly mood for conversation.

"They have healing powers. The giraffes. Good for the mantel. Spread peace to all in the house. See their long necks? They see far. Into the future. Can I help you?"

"I am not sure, I have not come to buy carvings," I said almost apologetically, "I am looking for an adoption agency that used to be, well, here?"

"Oh, I am sorry, I can't help you there," he said, looking at me intently. "As you can see, this is a curio store," he added, gesturing with his hands.

"Would you know where or what happened to the agency?"

"No idea. Sorry I can't help you."

"Yesterday the building was padlocked."

"Stock-taking. But if you're not interested in our sculptures, it should not concern you when and why we close."

"How long have you been open?" I asked him. "As a curio center, I mean?"

"Woman, are you some kind of police?" he asked rather aggressively. "Look, if you are not buying anything . . ." For some reason, he donned the mask of the charging rhino and made as if to charge me.

"No no, sorry for asking, very rude of me, thanks for your help," I said, retreating quickly.

"No trouble, ma'am," he growled through the mask.

Right before I crossed the street, I looked back. The man, with the rhino mask in his hand, was standing at the door, watching me. I waved, not knowing exactly why, and then got into my car and drove off. But the image of the man in a rhino mask stayed in my mind for a long time. In the image, the rhino mask had replaced the human head. The Rhino Man, he became in my mind.

I called Melinda and told her I had to see her. In no time, I was at her place in West Orange, New Jersey. The four-bedroom Melinda Palace, as she liked to call it, complete with a swimming pool, was off the main street but not visible from the road, because it was surrounded by trees. I threw my orange *kikoi,* which I used as a scarf, on the couch and delved right into the reason for my visit.

"Are you crazy?" Melinda asked, alarmed. "Why put your life in danger?"

"Couldn't help it. As it turns out, it's only a curio shop," I said. "Aren't you a little bit curious that I found it open so soon after we found it closed?"

"That's why it alarms me. How could an adoption agency turn out to be a curio shop in the course of a few weeks? And who talked to Zack? Who faxed him those papers?"

"My questions exactly. The adoption must exist someplace. Did you find anything in cyberspace? An online existence of Kasla?"

"No," she said. "I have tried all sorts of search engines, but nothing like that comes up. I will keep trying. But tell you what: Why don't you ask Zack? Talk it over with him candidly. If I were still married to Mark, I would also probe."

"Don't let it worry you. I have decided to quit this nonsense."

"Good."

"Unless Ben comes up with something substantial."

"Ben?" she asked.

"Oh, a police officer I knew as a student."

"You went to see the police?" she asked, sounding surprised.

"Yes, I did. In a personal way. I didn't want to alarm Zack with speculation."

"Oh, Mugure, aren't you taking this too far? Why bring the police into it?"

"I just told you. I went to see Ben as a friend."

"Perhaps I should put it more bluntly," Melinda said. "You don't know who else the police may be working for. The best of them give tips to newspapers and get paid for it. The Murdoch virus. I am not saying that Ben is like that. But I don't trust the police."

"Noted," I said. "But please, Melinda, this is between us, okay?"

"You know you can trust me."

Of course, I thought as I rushed to the car. I had to race

back in time to collect Kobi from school—a challenge, given the New York traffic—but I was lucky and managed to beat the afternoon rush. Melinda was right: I had to talk to Zack candidly, minus the bit about Ben.

During dinner, Zack asked after my day, as usual.

"It was okay," I said in a noncommittal tone.

"What did you do?"

"Well, I just . . . you know, the usual, with the girls, shopping, Kobi . . . that kind of thing. And you? How was your day?" I asked, trying to change the focus.

This would have been a good opening for the conversation I really wanted to have, but I waited until Kobi had gone to bed, when we were sitting in the living room. Zack made us glasses of gin and tonic. He beat me to the questions. "Someone said they saw you in Manhattan?"

I almost jumped out of my seat. "Manhattan, why, yes, I was looking for Tiffany's. That diamond necklace I have been threatening to buy. I couldn't find the branch I wanted and ended up lost in some deserted area. I will try again tomorrow."

"It's dangerous out there, you know," he said. "You really have to use your GPS and even then confine yourself to the city center. I am not so sure venturing into perilous areas is a good idea."

My frustrations welled up inside me, and something snapped. "Why are you giving me a lecture about safety?" I said. "I know my way well enough around the city. I was a student at CCNY for four years, remember?"

He stood up, came behind me, and put loving hands on my shoulders. "I am sorry, Mugure," he said, kissing my ear. "I've been out of sorts lately. I'm under too much pressure at work. I got really unsettled about the agency closing down. I just can't trace them. It's like they never existed."

"But, Zack, you talked to somebody. And that somebody sent you some material with wrong dates and names. You should be telling me how an adoption agency turns out to be a curio shop," I said, no longer disguising the fact that I was not taking him at his word.

"Curios?" he said, a little puzzled.

I told him that I had been to the premises.

"One cannot tell in these days of the Internet," he said. "Virtual offices. Outsourcing. Sometimes you get calls about products and services here in America, then you discover the call came from India. Cheaper that way."

In the back of my mind, I was hearing echoes of Melinda's words about virtual reality. "Melinda has looked into it. Kasla does not exist online," I told him.

"Please don't let it concern you. I will get to the bottom of this."

"Should we worry about it?" I asked him, more as a statement than a question.

He went back to his seat. "Legally, we have nothing to worry about. I did everything by the book. But you get to wondering, you know . . ."

I decided to tell him about Mark, my suspicions more or less confirmed by Melinda, and urged him to be extra-careful with his friends. I hoped that would make it easier for him to talk to me about his friendship with Mark or what he truly knew about Kobi's adoption.

"I am sorry to have added to your worries," I found myself saying, but no sooner did I let out the words than another thought crept in. Who had told Zack about my Manhattan trip? There were only three people who knew:

Melinda, Ben, and the Rhino Man. Ben had used the same words that Zack had used. The Rhino Man had looked hard at me; he had probably read my license number and traced it to me or Zack. Could Mark have seen and talked to Zack as his way of doing to my relationship what he thought I had done to his relationship with Melinda? Countless possibilities.

"Zack, who told you I was in Manhattan?"

"David," he said without hesitation.

I decided to quit playing amateur detective. It was not as if there had been any crime. It was foolish of me to persist in pointless obstinacy, unraveling a past that posed no threats to the present. Why should I disrupt my family stability to satisfy nothing? Sometimes ignorance is bliss.

Two days later, while I was sitting in my car waiting for Kobi to finish a soccer match and feeling good about my new resolve, my cell phone rang. It was Ben.

"Ben, how kind of you to check on me. How are you?" I said. "I must apologize for the other day. I am not sure what I was thinking. The good news is that I have decided to drop the whole matter. It's silly."

"That's very wise, Mugure," Ben said after a pause. "Well, then, I suppose the information I have is not necessary."

"What, wait, did you find something?" I said.

"It's not much, but sometime last year, the Kasla agency was under investigation for some unusual adoption procedures. No charges were filed. Police did not have enough evidence to prosecute. The agency folded up on its own. Your questions are not enough of a basis for us to reopen the file. Unless you—or someone else—were to come up with new evidence of a crime. But the fact that it was under investigation establishes that it did exist sometime in the past. I just wanted to let you that you were not chasing a ghost, exactly."

"Thank you, Ben. The information is interesting, but like you, I have closed the file."

"Don't you want to know the law firm that represented them?"

Ignorance is bliss, I told myself again, though there was no harm in knowing. "Who?" I asked.

"Edward and Palmer."

"What?" I shouted, pulling the phone from my ear to look at it. The tension in my cheeks tightened. Just then I saw Kobi running toward me. "Ben, I have to go. I will be in touch," I said, and hung up.

Kobi got in the car, excited by the goal he had scored. He took a ball we had bought him for home practice and hugged it. I tried to force a smile. I drove home, fighting to focus on Kobi's happiness and not the shock of Ben's revelation.

A few seconds later, the phone rang again. I pulled over to answer it.

That call would haunt me, follow me even in the Nairobi streets, sometimes wake me in the unexpected hours. I would recall my near certainty that it was Detective Underwood calling me again, perhaps to add to what he had told me. I would see and hear myself asking: "Hey, got more details?" The muffled noise and shallow breathing would come back, the questions ending with the threat, uttered so simply: "You are asking too many questions," almost like a warning from a friend. I would see myself arriving home, cold with fear, numerous questions popping up in my mind from nowhere.

They folded into one: Should I tell Zack? It was a question that I should not have had to ask, but the information that Ben had given me deepened my indecision: Tell Zack about the threat, or confront him about the links between his law firm and the mysterious Kasla agency?

I woke up the next morning tired and worried. Chaotic thoughts and images swirled in my mind; why did they want me to stop asking questions? It wasn't as if I had been all over the city, accosting each and every person I met. I went over any contact of whom I had asked questions recently or in the past. The voice was male. That ruled out Melinda. I was sure I would have recognized Joe's voice. The only other question was to the Rhino Man, and I didn't know how he would have gotten my number. Could Ben be playing games with me, disguising his voice or getting a fellow officer to do his dirty work? Messing with my mind? Who else might have an interest in toying with me? Mark. He had wagged a warning finger at me. He had recommended Kasla . . .

Kasla was at the center of my problems. Where was this ghostly agency that received telephone calls, faxed papers, and then retreated to the silence of the dead? And yet it did exist once, as Ben had confirmed: It had given us Kobi, and it had sought and received representation from Edward and Palmer. I had to crack the mystery. I did not tell Zack, but the resolution to handle the threats all by myself and at the same time steady my nerves was easier said than done.

Even Rosie noticed that I was out of sorts. I thought of

telling her the whole story, but then I felt uncomfortable dragging her into my increasingly troubled domestic life. It was as if she read my thoughts and beat me to it. I was in the garden when she came over and said after a few nothings: "My sister, I don't know what is worrying you. Please forgive me for saying it, but I don't like these white people around you. Me, I keep all white folk at arm's length. Is there anything I can do to lift your burden? Do you want to talk to your African sister?" I thanked her and told her all was well. Then I became suspicious; she had taken the same line as Ben on white people. I thought of asking her if she knew him or talked to him, then changed my mind.

I went back inside the house. A shot of vodka helped me relax a little and follow some threads of thought. Ben had told me they could reopen the Kasla file only if there were evidence of a crime. An unrecorded telephone threat was not a provable crime. The ghostly existence of an adoption agency was not a crime. But what if I could somehow procure the letters, briefs, emails, any correspondence between Edward and Palmer and the Kasla agency? I wished I could engage some clever hackers to break into the law files and retrieve the information I needed. Melinda had the reputation of being a master at computers, and she fancied herself an expert in cyber warfare, but I didn't think it wise to ask her. I could break into Zack's home office, but what if there was nothing there? What I needed was some basic facts with which to confront my husband and extract more information.

Mark kept on coming to mind. He must know Kasla. He had talked about business links to Africa, Kenya, oh yes, that night at the wedding. Without Melinda, there was no way of getting to him.

And then an idea dawned on me. My mother used to tell me the longest road was usually the shortest. I needed to locate the Kenya adoption agency with which Kasla had partnered. The partner agency in Kenya would lead me back to America.

6

Jane Kagendo came to mind. She had not come to our wedding because she'd been involved in a case involving alternative clinics. She was not at her desk when I phoned, but after ten minutes, she returned the call. I explained my situation. She had not heard of Kasla in Kenya or, for that matter, in New York, or any such partnership. Could she get me a list of all the registered adoption clinics in the country? I asked.

"I thought I was done with clinics, adoptive or otherwise, after my legal battles over Alternative Clinics," she said.

"Please, Jane, I just want adoption agencies," I said, a little embarrassed that I knew so little about her battles. The text she had sent us did not contain details about the case.

A day later, she emailed me a list of six registered agencies. Most were church-based, a few government- or quasi-government-managed. I called them all. Two agencies did not answer, but the other four said they had never heard of Kasla. The matter needed further investigation by someone on the ground. I felt uneasy at the thought of taking Jane from her serious work to pursue a whim. Then Wainaina came to mind.

I was in my last year at CCNY when I met him at an NYU lecture on technology, philosophy, and the new media by a famous Harvard professor; it was part of a summer workshop on globalization and the social media. In his arguments for a universal ethical imperative, the professor quoted Immanuel Kant, first in German and then in English: "Act only according to that maxim whereby you can, at the same time, will that it should become a universal law." I did not understand the jargon, and I suspect I was not alone, but we all were completely mesmerized by his sonorous delivery.

Amid the respectful silence, a young man raised his hand. There was total silence when I whispered to the woman next to me: "He has a body to die for." The man with the cordless mike happened to be passing it and must have had it on, because my comment was caught by a live mike. Laughter broke out. I felt like disappearing in a hole. I tried to laugh along with everybody else to hide my embarrassment. The young man was not flustered.

"The only problem, sir, is that you seem to assume the universal ethical imperative resides in the West, a white platonic model to be copied or mimicked by Africa and Asia," he said, and sat down amid murmuring.

Though the professor was expecting a question that sought his wisdom and not a comment that questioned his assumptions, he maintained his calm. The young man's courage impressed me, and after the lecture, I sought him. Sponsored by his newspaper, he had come from Kenya just for the summer workshop. We exchanged phone numbers, and I called him a few times, but our communication gradually dwindled to zero.

I called the *Daily Star,* the paper that had sent him, and luckily, I got him. "The man with a body to die for," I started by way of introduction. He laughed and remembered me, expressing regret that we had communicated so little. He was just finishing up an article on an investigation, but he promised to get right back to me.

When he did, I went straight to the point, but like Jane, he had never heard of Kasla. I asked if he could find out about the two agencies who had not answered my calls. I gave him the names. He did not ask many questions.

Two days later, Wainaina called me. "Well, one of the agencies has been closed for a few years now. The other is a children's homeless shelter that doubles as an adoption agency, Three Ms. Their logo is a pair of eyeglasses."

He did not have the names of the owners but said he would look them up in the registry and get back to me. Nothing much, I thought, except for the logo. Even with this, I brushed aside Melinda's cautionary advice, got on the phone with Ben, and asked to meet him. Even I could see that the information from Jane and Wainaina was not breaking news, but I wanted any excuse to urge Ben to have the file on Kasla opened and ask if he could give me more details about the Palmer and Kasla connection before I confronted Zack.

Twenty minutes later, Ben was sitting across from me at a Starbucks close to his precinct in the Bronx. As he munched his croissant with his coffee, I told him what I had garnered so far, and my hopes.

"I see where you are going with this," Ben said, looking at me quizzically. "The Kasla file, as I told you, has been closed. We can't chase ghosts, suspicions, and gossip. Mu-gure, what are you really looking for? You aren't cut out for this investigative stuff. It could mean trouble."

"Don't you think I know that? Why do you think I am coming to you?"

"You don't have anything concrete. Names of agencies in Kenya with eyeglasses for logos? A little piece of paper with your child's name written on the back is not exactly evidence of a kidnapping ring. "

"I have not said a thing about rings and kidnapping," I said, my frustration and irritation matching his skepticism. "What about the threats? The phone call warning me to stop asking questions? At the very least, you can investi-gate how the Kasla premises became a curio shop."

"I don't know." He paused and looked at me again, and it dawned on me what he was implying.

"Are you saying I lied about that phone call?" I asked in a slightly tremulous voice.

"No, no. It's not that. But I have to be candid. I told you about Edward and Palmer representing Kasla. What has Zack told you about it? Quite frankly, I thought that was why you wanted to see me."

I felt his scrutiny: It was as if I were under investigation. I felt foolish and awkward. "I have not yet talked to him about it."

"Why? It would seem his responses would be a good starting point. Charity begins at home, that kind of thing. What about the telephone threat? Have you talked to him about it?"

"I thought I'd dig up a few facts first. I hoped you would give me a few concrete details. Something written, for in-stance. I did not want to spread fear to the entire family."

"Shall I talk to him about it?" he suddenly asked, ignoring my requests.

"Ben, I know you are trying to be helpful," I said in a conciliatory tone. "I will talk to him myself. I am sure he will tell me everything about the Edward and Palmer connection. And what he does not know, he can dig up in the firm's archives. I promise to share with you whatever I find out. But leave it to me. For now."

He stood there looking at me in a way that he had not done before. His unfinished croissant gaped up like a fish's pouting mouth. He was about to say something and then changed his mind, got up, and walked away slowly, as if debating whether to come back or simply continue. I sat there, confused. Was I going crazy? I got up and ordered another coffee, a venti, and sipped it slowly.

Oh God, I was picking up Kobi from school, I remembered. In a panic, I looked at the time and realized I had fifteen minutes to get there. I ran over to the car, some meters from the café. I was backing out when I saw a car come out of nowhere. I tried to step on the gas and engage first gear to move forward again, out of the way. It was too late. BOOM. Darkness.

I woke up in a strange place. I could barely make out the figures surrounding my bed except their white overcoats.

"She's coming around," I heard someone say.

It took me a while to figure out that I was in a hospital bed, surrounded by a doctor and nurses. My head felt as if it were a bag of heavy metal attached to my body and rattling when I moved. The collision came back to me. I tried to get up but felt a sharp pain on my side. "Kobi! I must get him from school, I must—"

"Take it easy," a familiar voice said.

It was Zack. Thank God. He bent and hugged me. "How are you feeling?" he asked.

"Sore. All over."

"I'm glad you are not seriously injured. No broken ribs, says the doctor, but what happened?" he asked.

"I remember backing out and seeing a car come straight toward me," I said as the day's events became clearer.

"You think they did it on purpose?" Zack asked, looking puzzled.

"Zack, it was not an accident," I said.

"I hope the police catch him."

I said nothing. The concern in his voice made me feel guilty about the doubts I harbored. The guilt followed me home. I was grateful that I was not badly hurt. Kobi's joyful smile was enough to lighten the ache and the gloom.

I thought about Ben. Minutes after our first meeting in his office, I'd gotten the phone threat. I had made the sensible decision to quit. Then, out of the blue, he'd volunteered some information that led to our meeting at Starbucks. Moments after our meeting, a car had hit me. In my mind, I went over his glances, gestures, and silences. To Ben, I was a black damsel imprisoned in a white castle. Could he try to accomplish his self-avowed mission by scaring me, making me suspicious of Zack, bringing about an irrevocable division between man and wife? How could I trust the story about Edward and Palmer?

I must tell Zack everything. Yes. Build trust. Then ask him about Palmer and the Kasla agency. The heart-to-heart must take place on a day when he was not going to the office. The weekend of my return was the best time to unburden myself. Rosie had offered to take Kobi for the weekend to give me space.

On Saturday, Zack attended a fund-raiser to which we had been invited. We agreed he would make an appearance, offer excuses for me, and come back quickly. The fact was, I was scared to be left home alone. Sensing my fears, Zack asked me to lock the entire house from the inside.

He called every half hour till I told him he should not have gone to the event if he was going to spend every minute checking up on me. But his solicitous calls quelled my lingering doubts about him and increased my determination to confess everything.

I was watching the nightly news when I heard a car in the driveway. My heart skipped a beat. I quickly switched off the TV and picked up the phone, ready to hit the 911 button. I crawled on all fours toward the kitchen, grabbed a kitchen knife, and went to the window to peep. It was a police car. Relief. Speak of the devil. Ben was standing right outside my door and pressing the bell. I put the knife down where I could reach it quickly if needed. Then I opened the door.

"Ben, you should have called to say you were coming. I was going to stab you with a kitchen knife," I said. "Can I get you something to drink?" I gestured for him to take a seat.

"Yes, some water would be nice."

I pulled a bottle from the fridge and gave it to him along with a glass. I watched him carefully as he took the first sip.

"I came to tell you we caught the guy who hit you," he said.

"You did?"

He looked at my anxious self and smiled. "Well, let's see," he started, as if amused by a thought. "He is seventy-five years old, with bad eyesight. He lives in the nursing home up the block from the café. This man stole the car from the nursing home. He is not supposed to drive, and his mental condition is questionable. You'll think this is bizarre, but he escaped from the scene of your accident only to crash again thirty minutes later on the New Jersey Turnpike, heading to Newark." He broke into a smile. "Remarkable for a guy that old, on medication, who usually cannot see beyond his nose." He drank the rest of the water.

Ben left me with more questions than answers. Did he expect me to believe that cock-and-bull story? I called Zack but felt silly, and instead of telling him to come home, which was what I wanted, I said, "Honey, just calling to assure you I'm fine, and to tell you that I love you. Have a good time."

7

I should have told him about my fears, I thought as soon as I hung up. The more I revisited Ben's story, the more tense I became. I checked the doors and windows to make sure they were all secure. I pulled down the blinds and switched on the lights in all the rooms to suggest multiple human presences. I wondered if I should go for Zack's gun, but I quickly dismissed the thought: Even if I could access it, I had never used a gun. I kept the kitchen knife near the sofa.

My other friend, gin and tonic, was beckoning me, but I decided against the foolishness. I had to remain fully alert for whatever would follow Ben's departure. I decided coffee would calm my nerves. Drink it slowly. Yes, and perhaps watch a DVD. I had bought a few of *The Real Housewives of New Jersey* but had not had the time to watch any, given that I was chasing "criminals."

I put on the coffee machine and then inserted the DVD. I recalled the episode in the film *Home Alone* when Macaulay Culkin, playing Kevin McCallister, wards off intruders by turning on the TV: "Get the hell out of here," the TV character threatens, his voice followed by the sound of gunfire. The intruders trip over themselves in flight. I did not expect gunfire in the DVD, but I thought the conversation might deter an intruder. I increased the volume.

I needed to use the bathroom, though. I pressed the pause button. I was coming back to my seat when I heard a car outside. "Oh, no, not the Ben thing again," I said as I picked up the kitchen knife. The intruder tried the door handle first and then rang the bell. I held my breath. I heard him trying a key. I gripped the knife with grim determination. He pushed the door open . . .

"Zack!" I said, and let go of the knife. I felt tears at the edges of my eyes as I clung to him with a mixture of relief and remorse all the way to the sofa. "Hold me tight, Zack," I said, as if to convince myself that all was well.

"What were you doing with the knife?" he asked, trying to calm me and probably himself.

"Zack," I said, slightly distraught, "I wanted you to come home right away. Then I felt silly and said the opposite of what I truly felt!"

"The tone of your voice betrayed you," Zack said. "The tremor told me you were trying to control your fear. So I left the party and drove home like a madman."

"Thank you, Zack. They say the man was unstable."

"Who? What are you talking about?"

"Ben was here," I said.

"I don't understand."

"I'm sorry. Please make me a gin and tonic."

Ever the gentleman, he made two. "Okay, what is it, Mugure?"

I told him about Ben's visit and the story he had spun

about a mentally unstable seventy-five-year-old, successfully hijacking a car from a nursing home and hitting me.

"Oh my, really?" said Zack. "I am glad they caught him."

"But do you believe the story?"

"Why not?'

"Zack, I don't trust Ben."

"Why? He is your friend. You introduced him to me."

I realized that to tell him why, I would have to talk about the pattern of bad things that followed each encounter with Ben. That would mean disclosing the prior meetings with Ben and the doubts that had led to them. I realized I was not quite ready to tell all.

"I don't think Ben approved of my marrying you, a white guy. He has strong views on black pride."

"Look, Mugure. I don't know Ben very well, but I don't think he would go that far. Whatever his racist private views are, he is a sworn public servant. You can't jump to conclusions on the basis of a story."

"Zack, why are you always protecting people?" I was going to give the example of Mark and then stopped.

"Mugure. Let's make it simple. I will find out whether the story is true. We are a big firm, and we have our contacts."

"Zack, thank you."

I felt relief and afterward tried to see the positive side of Ben's visit. I had been able to tell Zack of my fears without having to disclose everything. I could build on it without having to start from the beginning.

Zack was true to his word. The following evening he came home with what he or his people had been able to find out.

"It's true, Mugure. Apparently, the man died on the way to the hospital."

"Oh," I said, not knowing how to react.

I was relieved. Zack seized on that and tried to make me laugh by filling me in on the party the night before, dwelling on the famous twins who had dominated our wedding. The whole idea of designer twins—the version that always got people's attention—was so ridiculous that I had to laugh every time Zack told the story, even now.

The talk drifted to stories of the many women who had surgical alterations in order to look like a Barbie doll. Imagine if real body parts were made to order and customized to meet the different idiosyncrasies; wouldn't such women flock to the market? It was grotesque humor, but it somehow made me laugh before we retired to bed and, for the first time in a little while, made love. I did not reach the heavens, as before.

Though I did not tell him, my every caress was an unspoken promise to give up digging up the truth about Kobi's past, to let go whatever it was that Zack, Melinda, Ben, and my good sense had urged me to let go.

Come to think of it, what exactly had I been looking for? An answer to why there had been some contradictory information about Kobi? And what was it that had me all worked up? The closure of Kasla? Its transformation into a curio shop? There was the strange phone call and then the car accident, but the call may have been a prank, and the car accident had been explained. When all was said and done, the fact remained that I had not heard by hint or rumor the slightest negative thing about Kobi's adoption.

For the next few days, I confined myself to the house and to taking Kobi to school, soccer games, and slumber parties. Whenever the phone rang, I checked the caller ID and answered only Zack's or Rosie's calls. I was not bored.

TV programs kept me company; I watched enough *Roots* reruns to last me a lifetime. I didn't like repetitive opinion journalism, but I was hooked on *The Rachel Maddow Show*. She had a tongue that bit; a tone that stung; and a smile that softened the bite and the sting.

It was during this time that I began to enjoy being in the house alone, dressing how I liked, and when Rosie was not around, even walking about nude. Mostly, I wore see-through tops and blue jeans and watched Oprah go on about living one's best life. A remarkable woman. I often wondered how she had made it in a white world and how she felt having such a large following of white people eating out of her hands.

Suddenly, as I went back to the living room to watch *Oprah*, I felt the weight of the emptiness in the house. I missed Kobi and Zack. I couldn't wait to pick up Kobi and hear all about his latest adventures. I felt a chill. Then I caught sight of Zack's coat hanging by the hall closet. I walked over and put it on, then turned the coffee machine on. Coffee would give me one kind of warmth; his coat, another. At that moment I wanted him to hold me tight, tight, and never let me go, squeeze out all my doubts. I held the jacket close to me.

I liked its smell, the smell of Zack, and in it, I felt at one with him. I put my hands in the pockets, like he usually did, and walked like he usually did, hands in the coat pockets. My right hand felt some paper. I pulled it out. It had "Mark" scribbled on it and then crossed out.

"Honey?" I heard Zack calling as he opened the door and entered.

Were I not so upset, I would have appreciated the fun in the situation: me standing there, dressed like him! But

I was seething with anger, so I just stood there looking at him, not knowing where to start.

"So . . . Mark, huh?" I grunted, throwing the tiny piece of paper at him.

It floated in the air briefly and then landed at his feet. He stood still. He seemed afraid—well, more confused. Then he bent down and picked it up and read it. I didn't want to scream and shout, but I came close. I could feel myself shaking. "What's going on between you and Mark?" I asked coldly.

He didn't say anything but put his briefcase down and wiped his forehead with his forearm. It may have been caused by his slow reaction, but something inside me broke.

"Zack, you must tell me everything. About the gunman who once threatened you at the club, about your relationship with Melinda, about Alaska Enterprises. Do you understand? Everything! That is, if you want this marriage to survive. And don't take me as completely ignorant. No, Zack. You are making a mistake, a big mistake, to underestimate me. I know that Edward and Palmer was retained by Kasla."

He stood there, almost frozen. He walked toward the kitchen. I followed him. He pulled out a kitchen chair and slumped in it. He pointed at another chair and mumbled for me to sit. I did, not because I wanted to but because I was feeling weak in the knees. I had to be strong.

"Let's talk," he said. "I was going to bring up much of what you just raised later on, but now is as good a time as any. You have to believe me. That gunman. I honestly don't know him. I had never seen him before or since. I just took his gun-toting craziness as case of mistaken identity. As for the agency and our law firm, we are a big enterprise with many branches. Not all the lawyers in a firm know each and every case, because most cases don't go beyond the letter-writing stage. I told you I would get to the bottom of this. I only recently—actually, the day of your accident—learned that the agency had retained my firm. One letter from the firm, with all the weight our name carries, was enough to make the state desist. Which means it was not a case that generated much talk in the office. I am still looking into it. That and the whole Kasla saga."

Zack came across as sincere and forthright. There wasn't much more I could ask. Ben had given me so little, and Wainaina had not come up with anything extra from Kenya. Besides, I didn't want to rant about Ben. Let me keep my sources to myself, I resolved.

"About Mark," he continued. "I have been thinking hard about Mark, but I don't know, I really don't know. I think you might have been right."

"Why? What made you see the light?" I said as I leaned back, feeling a twinge of excitement. I couldn't help enjoying a little sense of superiority. "Better repent late than never," I told him.

"I am not sure about repenting," Zack responded. "But here it is: Mark would like me to join his venture. You know how he talks big. He did it at our wedding, remember? At first the proposal looked clean, you know, from a legal point of view." He looked at me and, seeing my slightly puzzled face, said, "Maybe I should start from the beginning. Mark would like me to be his business partner. He first approached me last year. He wants me to come in as the legal secretary for this multimillion-dollar land-scaping company to be based in the big cities of Africa: Cairo, Lagos, Johannesburg, Nairobi. Yes, in Nairobi. But

I don't know, something doesn't ring right. Landscaping in Africa?" He paused and looked at me. "Anyway, after what Melinda told you, and after reviewing the contents of a file he gave me, I am not so sure I want to go along."

"Why? What's in the file?"

"Nothing really alarming. Transaction papers, receipts, that kind of thing. A few items to sign if I agree. But it doesn't feel right. I can't afford to take chances right now, what with the cases I'm working on. And this Kasla business, I'm still trying to dig up facts . . . see if it was operating as a virtual office . . . it takes time, effort, and it's not as if I'm taking a holiday from my other duties as the firm's top international business attorney . . . I don't know, honey, I really don't know."

"There's no buts, no don't knows, about it," I said, sounding more stern than I felt. "Give up Mark, or he will mark you and yours for life." The fact was, I was relieved. That which would have come between us was gone. Now we would work it out together, man and wife.

"You know the funny thing?" he said. "Mark thought I would readily join because you come from Kenya!"

"Let him find another Melinda to torture," I said. I was glad that patience had paid off. I wanted and willed the doubts to vanish forever. Family first, I pledged in silence. My relief, written all over me, was a contrast to his obvious fatigue, as if the soul baring had been very demanding. "Don't look so morose," I said, trying to cheer him.

"There are other things weighing on me," he said, and let out a sigh. "I didn't want to burden you with bad news, but my friend David was picked up by undercover police earlier today."

"What? Why?" I asked, shocked.

"We don't know. A colleague has been assigned to follow up on it. But up till the time I left the office, the police would not say in what precinct he was being held."

"David is a good man," I said, and then I remembered Zack telling me that David had reported seeing me in Manhattan. "Might this affect you?"

"No, no, it probably has to do with some case. David was our top immigration lawyer. Probably detained by Homeland Security, but I'm only guessing, and a lawyer should not speculate. They raided his office and took many files. But we are a big firm with many good connections, and we shall get him out. It's just that he's a friend, my childhood friend."

We talked a lot that evening, and as he poured his heart out, I realized that the stress from his workplace was taking a toll on him, and all for the sake of Kobi and me. I had not been making it easy for him.

He told me more about his impending travel to Estonia and his mission to the other states formerly under Soviet communism as new frontiers for company business. He had also planned trips to Norway, Denmark, Sweden, and Finland. But if I felt I could not handle being alone with Kobi and Rosie, he offered to cancel the whole trip. "No, no," I said, "I won't hear of it." I felt I had sort of neglected him, what with my mind and energies focused on other things. From that evening and in the days before his travel to Estonia, I would make up for all the lost time.

On the eve of his trip, we went to Shamrock, the place that marked the beginning of our love journey. We danced to all of Melinda's songs. We were enjoying ourselves so much that when Melinda said she was performing her last song for the night, I felt cheated. Where had all the hours gone? As had become a habit, we went to her changing room. "Great show," I said as I hugged her.

"I am so tired. I kept hoping nobody would notice."

"No, you were great, as usual. I was stuck to the dance floor even after your last note," I said, laughing. "It's a pity you don't sing on bigger stages, in the biggest clubs."

"It's okay. It suits me fine. Plus, I get my compensation when I perform abroad. I am off to Rio, and then a few days later—guess what, Mugure?—I have a big gig coming up in Kenya. A performance at a festival, a kind of African or Kenyan version of a street carnival. They call it the Festival of Rags."

"That is wonderful, Melinda," I said, really happy for her. "I wish I could come with you, though I have never heard about the festival."

"It celebrates life's journey," Melinda said, "modeled, I assume, on the medieval Feast of Fools or the Belfast Festival of Fools. I don't care, I just want a chance to perform in Nairobi and Kisumu and Mombasa afterward."

"Congratulations, girl, you are moving on up," Zack said.

"Damn sure," she joked.

It was great that these two had remained friends with mutual respect, I thought. I was in high spirits. It was as if their going away to different parts of the world would remove them from the scene of my recent doubts and, in doing so, give me the space to erase the doubts and heal. Hand in hand, Zack and I stepped out of Shamrock as if readying for a new beginning.

I rejoiced too soon.

The suited gunman was waiting at the door. He held

the barrel of his gun to Zack's ribs. I took a step back and let out a whimper.

"You scream again, I silence you."

"Leave her out of this," Zack appealed. "We can settle this between us. What do you want?"

It was eerie, we three standing in the middle of Forty-Second Street, the neon lights all around us, cars passing, humans, too, and yet none of the dwellers in the city that never sleeps cast a glance in our direction.

"Message from the Priest. Nothing in his vaults lately. Must have the *original* document. You have proved unworthy of keeping it. From the moment you land in Estonia and onward, his eyes are on you. Last warning."

Again, just like that, the suited gunman vanished among the passing crowds. Relieved despite my shaking, I turned to Zack. He was frantically ferreting in his pockets, particularly the inside of the coat. He bent down and did the same inside his socks. I felt he was looking at all the places he could have hidden a gun. This time he was clearly shaken, if unsuccessfully trying to control himself. "Don't worry," he told me, trying to reassert his wounded pride. "You can sum up a lawyer's life in four words: clients, courts, money, and documents."

"Who is the Priest?" I asked, as if I had not noted the murderous rage and Zack's desperate search for a gun he did not have.

"Obviously, his code for a generic client," he said. "It's a case of mistaken identity."

"Twice the man has held a gun to your head. A misunderstanding, maybe, but mistaken, I don't know," I said with as much calm as I could muster.

"I will look into it. But I am sure he has his messages mixed up."

"Let's report it to the police."

"We don't have anything concrete to report. And I am leaving tomorrow morning. After my trip, I will crack the case," he said.

I did not want a fight on the eve of his departure. The gun thing worried me, but I assumed it must worry him more. It was another burden on top of the detention of David West.

8

I drove Zack to Kennedy airport. Normally, he took a cab. Today I was not taking chances. I was determined not to leave the area until I was sure the plane had taken off safely. I had forgotten that this was post-9/11 and I could not follow him beyond the departure gate. So I walked back slowly and ordered a cup of mocha at a Starbucks and sat in a corner with my eyes glued to the huge screen that showed departures and arrivals.

"May I join you, sister?"

I turned around, tensed up. I let out a sigh of relief. "Ben, what are you doing here? You don't have to ask."

He sat opposite me; he'd ordered a mocha, too, as if in unspoken solidarity. He was in his dashiki, looking every inch the casual traveler. "I happened to be out here, and I said to myself, What a coincidence. I had been thinking of coming to see you."

"About what?" I said.

"You! To see how you are!"

"I am fine. I feel fine. My would-be killer is dead, you told me."

"Mugure, it turns out the man, whoever he was, is not dead. He is still out there. There was a car crash on the New Jersey Turnpike, but it had nothing to do with your accident."

"What are you talking about? You or your officers confirmed the death to Zack."

"Although we believed your story, we had to fool them. So we put out a false story to make them believe the police had been fooled."

"They? Who are they?"

"How well do you know Zack's friends?" he asked, making me wonder if those friends were part of "they." Zack's circle of friends was small. There was Mark. There was David. There were Joe and Melinda.

"I won't say I do," I said vaguely, noncommittal. "What about the ones you were trying to fool?"

"I don't know if it's one or more, frankly, but we are trying to figure that out. And the motive. It's obvious that the man had seen us together. He must have thought you gave information to the police. Information they did not want given. We have not yet found the motive, but be assured, we shall not rest until we apprehend the man."

"Ben, you told me I had nothing to worry about. Meanwhile, a man after my life is still out there. And you? What are you doing at the airport? Following me? Tell me the truth, am I in danger?" I asked getting agitated.

"You will have to tell me."

"What do you mean?"

"I don't know if you remember, but I once told you that I do detective work on the remains of 9/11. It's my belief that the whole truth about the non-Caucasians who perished has not been told." At that point, I lost track of Ben.

He didn't even acknowledge my baffled look as he continued explaining. "I have been tracking down somebody who I believe has information that might help me. I have reason to believe that you know the man."

"You are crazy. I have nothing to do with 9/11. I have never visited the site, even. Is that why you are following me?" I wondered if Ben had finally lost it. What were all these theories? What was he talking about?

"Calm down, Mugure. I was following the man."

"The man who tried to kill me?"

"No, the man who accosted you and your husband outside Shamrock. Last night."

"The suited gunman?"

"That fits the description, yes. Please, Mugure, tell me what happened."

The whole thing sounded eerie, bizarre. I controlled my trembling with difficulty. I had nothing to hide. I told him everything about the two altercations with the suited gunman.

"The document. The Priest. Deposits? That's all?"

"Except that last night he upped the threat. He said he would keep an eye on Zack in Estonia. He seemed to know something about Zack, but Zack did not seem to know anything about the gunman. You said you were following the man. Where is he?"

Ben let out a sigh. His gaze never left me. It was as if he wanted to read my every expression and gesture. "The suited gunman, as you call him, just boarded the flight to Estonia."

"No!" I almost screamed. "He is going to kill my husband."

"Listen, Mugure. We have our eyes everywhere. I will

give you my number, my very private number. Memorize it. Promise that if you see or sense anything suspicious, you'll call me. But please be careful. Be wary of the circle of friends. Do this! Don't act as if you know and trust everything about them," he cautioned, and left.

I called Melinda, hoping that she had not left. I wanted to meet so I could share my fear. She had not left, she said. Then I changed my mind and simply told her that Zack had left and I was once again a single parent. She was leaving the following day, she bubbled with happiness. "Let's get together for girl talk," she said. No, I did not want to interfere with her preparations. "Have a nice trip to Rio," I said. "And Nairobi," she reminded me. Festival of Rags.

I drove slowly, turning over Ben's revelations in my mind. The man who had tried to hit me was alive and well and roaming the streets of New York. The suited gunman was on the flight with Zack. I wasn't sure whether to believe Ben's version of events—his conspiracy theories. If the suited gunman had gone after Zack, why didn't Ben seem all that worried? Then I recalled David in custody. I should have asked Ben why he had been detained and whether it had anything to do with Zack.

The traffic on the Van Wyck from Kennedy was extremely heavy and slow, which suited my present mood. I went straight to school and collected Kobi. As it usually did, his smile cheered me. He was the best thing to happen in my life. The day's issue of the *City News* was at the door, along with an envelope. Kobi took the newspaper and handed me the envelope, addressed to Mr. and Mrs. Zack

Sivonen. It must have been hand-delivered, for there were no postal marks. There was a poorly scribbled "Enjoy!" on the envelope, which held a DVD. In the lounge, I slid the disk into the player. Some fuzzy bits came up and then a shadowy figure. My heart skipped a beat. Wait a minute, that was me, walking toward the door of the curio shop, the site of the ghostly Kasla. More fuzzy bits came up, and then I was sitting at Starbucks, waiting for Ben on the day of the accident.

Blood rushed to my head. I felt prickly heat under my arms. Whoever dropped off this DVD must have seen Zack and me go to the airport. He or she must have been prowling around our house. I looked about. Then I felt a presence. I swung around only to find Kobi staring at me.

"Mommy, what are you doing in the video?"

"Video? What video?"

"The one we have been watching. Who took it? They should take one of me going to school or playing soccer."

"I don't know," I murmured.

I felt trapped with indecision. Zack was on the plane. Melinda was going away. I had to do something. My enemies were following my every move. Could it be Mark, now angry that Zack had rejected his shady schemes? And he would know that Zack was going to Estonia, Melinda was away, and I was home alone. Or maybe it was the gunman. But he was somewhere in the sky. I thought of the hotline to Ben. Once again, something had happened soon after I met with him. He was a suspect. And he knew that Zack was out of town.

I was no longer undecided: Kobi and I had to get out of the house. I ran upstairs to my room and grabbed our passports—the essentials, as I called them—then ran to his

room, shoved some of his games, toys, and clothes in a
duffel bag, and ran back downstairs.

"What's wrong?" he asked.

"Nothing, dear, let's go to the car," I said, hardly able
to calm my voice.

I was not sure exactly where to go. All I knew and felt
was that I had to get out of the Bronx, be anywhere but the
Bronx. I drove in a hypnotic state.

"Where are we going, Mommy?"

I glanced at the clock in the car. I had been driving in a
dazed state for some time.

"Belle Haven," Kobi read out, his way of trying to figure out where I was taking us. He was good at directions;
he liked reading signposts out loud. It was then that I realized we were on Interstate 95 and I had been driving
toward Joe's house.

"To Uncle Joe's," I told Kobi, as if that had been my
intended destination all along.

"Okay," he said with doubt, and went back to his
Game Boy.

I drove up to the iron gates and rang the bell, hoping Joe was not out on a date. I was grateful when the
gates started opening but even more so when I drove up
the hill and saw Joe's red sports car parked outside the
house.

Kobi and I made our way through the marble pillars on
either side of the door to the mansion. It was so good to
see him standing at the door. "What are my favorite people
doing here?" he said as he hugged me.

"We came up to check on you."

"Come in, come in," he said.

As we stepped on the ceramic tile floor, I marveled at

the high ceiling. We walked by two spiral staircases to the second floor and into his gourmet kitchen.

"How come you are home?" I asked.

"Believe it or not, I do spend some time alone," he said, pointing at something cooking on the stove. We laughed.

Later on, after Kobi had run off to the game room, I told Joe a slightly edited but largely true account of my recent adventures, including the DVD scare. I left out Ben and the shadow of the gunman. A shocked Joe continued staring even after I had finished.

"You mean to tell me someone has been stalking you? "

"Obviously," I replied, digging into my bag and waving the DVD.

He took the DVD, looked at it, and then gave it back. "Was there anything else in the envelope?"

"No."

"And what is this Alaska?" he asked me.

"Mark's company, probably, the one he talked about on the night of the wedding. I am sure that Mark blames me for Zack's refusal to join him in the venture, as he did for his divorce with Melinda. He bears me a grudge."

"Mark's a nice guy, he is just edgy, what with all the illegal Hispanics he employs," he said. "I don't think he and adoption centers would go hand in hand."

"He suggested the Kasla agency."

"Yes, I remember you trying to thank him and Mark refusing the honor."

"Almost as if he did not want a public acknowledgment."

"I don't know, people have many sides. I cannot vouch for anybody a hundred percent. Even Zack," he said, looking at me as if the last part had just come out.

"I can vouch for Zack," I shot back.

"I'm sorry. It's just my hunch about Mark. But I cannot swear for him in a court of law," Joe said.

Strange, but his words echoed the advice Ben had given me at the airport. Are they in communication? I thought.

"I am not here to talk about Mark or Zack or anybody," I said. "I am on the run from whoever placed this on our doorstep. I need a place for Kobi and me to shelter before I figure out the next step. I have many questions I need to sort out. But mostly, I want to know why they are afraid of me."

He said we were welcome to stay in his place until Zack returned. The two of them would follow up and make sure everything was okay. Even hire a private investigator if necessary.

I felt a huge boulder had been lifted off my shoulders. I started relaxing. Joe's sunny personality had that effect. After dinner, I tucked Kobi into bed in a guest room next to mine and rejoined Joe downstairs.

"Now, why the hell didn't you come into my life earlier, my love?" Joe asked lightheartedly as he sipped his cognac while I held a huge mug of hot chocolate.

"Zack beat you to it," I said. "And you'll agree he is more handsome."

"Handsome? He has the face; I have the muscle," he said, laughing and flexing his biceps. "But some women are attracted to vulnerable souls. Wounded souls, shall I say."

"Zack never went to war," I said, deliberately misunderstanding him.

"But Estonia has always been a battlefield. The Danes, Germans, Russians, Swedes, and even the Poles fought for control of this prime estate between the East and the West.

A kind of beautiful rug on which to rest their feet or wipe them. The Estonians have been victims of Nazi and, after it, Soviet rule. Independence 1991. Wars leave scars on the combatants in the battlefield of history."

"Zack is an Estonian American," I said. "Brought up here. Never tasted war. Didn't fight in Vietnam (too young), Iraq (too old), or any other American wars."

"Same with me," Joe said. "But what do you know of his father, grandfather, grandmother, and all the others before him? Trauma can be passed on to the next generation. Sins of our fathers kind of thing. I believe his grandfather would have been a young person during the Nazi occupation."

"It's funny you should say that," I said, warming to the subject. "Zack's father looked for his father, Zack's grandfather. He gave up. Zack didn't care for his father; he complained that Eha neglected the family for a dreamland and then the bottle. Zack has never explained what it was that turned his own father from the quest for his past to burying that past in liquor."

It felt good. Joe was the only one with whom I could discuss Zack's family dynamics, some at least, without a sense of betrayal.

Joe became serious. "From what Zack told me once, what Eha finally found in an obscure archive in Poland or Russia was a parchment containing his father's scribblings. It was a mix of Darwinism, Hinduism, Platonism, and good old feudalism. Nature is built on a succession of lower and higher forms. The lower nourish the higher. Grass feeds deer. Deer feeds lion. That kind of thing. Same for humans. The lower serves the higher. Destiny."

"Did the grandfather mean that higher-placed humans

could feed on the lower-placed humans? Cannibalism?" I asked.

Joe laughed, a big bellyful of laughter, repeating the word "cannibalism" several times. "Cannibalism is enshrined in the Christian order, you know. The holy Communion. The Eucharist. Drink my blood, eat my body, that kind of thing. I am a Roman Catholic, but I never received Communion. I don't agree with any form of cannibalism. I cautioned Zack against wasting much time on man-eat-man tendencies even if they come disguised as religion, philosophy, or some sort of idealism. I do believe in one cannibalism, though."

"Which is?"

"'Flesh on Flesh.' Mutual cannibalism," he said, and laughed again.

That was typical Joe. From the serious to the frivolous, and there was no point in trying to return him to the serious. Eventually, after more chitchat about nothing, we decided to turn in. "You know where to find stuff," he called as I got up to retire.

Zack and I had been here enough times that I knew where the bedding was kept. Before sleeping, I tried to call Zack, but his phone was off. I wondered if he had arrived in Estonia and whether he had encountered the suited gunman.

I felt safe here and slept like a baby. But later, I woke up to some noise in the kitchen. I sat up and looked at the clock. It was almost midday. I jumped out of bed and went to check Kobi's room. His bed was empty.

"Kobi? Joe?" I called out.

They were not in the kitchen, either. I walked into the lounge and found the French doors open. I heard some giggles coming from outside. And what a sight! Joe and Kobi were splashing in the pool. "Why don't you join us?" asked a beaming Joe.

"She has no bathing suit on," Kobi answered, clearly bemused.

"You can jump in with all your clothes on, we won't care, right, Kobi?"

I just smiled and sprawled on a lounge chair. "You guys should have woken me up."

"Your breakfast is in the kitchen," Joe said.

Joe went away to attend to some business, leaving Kobi and me to entertain ourselves. Kobi was beside himself as he went between swimming, Game Boy, and video games. "Joe is the bestest uncle in the whole world," he would say at intervals.

Later, I made dinner for three. Exhausted from all the excitement, Kobi ate early, so by the time Joe returned, he was fast asleep. After dinner, Joe and I retired to the lounge. He opened a bottle of wine, and we got to chatting, in between calls to and from his women.

"How do your girlfriends stand these phone calls?" I asked.

"They don't. That's why they all leave me after a while."

"Do you get lonely?"

"Sometimes," he said, looking straight ahead. "But you know, I am not the settling kind. I would get bored. If I were with you, it would be different."

"Oh, Joe, you would have tossed me aside after two months."

"No, you are different. I hope Zack knows and appreciates his Cleopatra. Otherwise, here comes Mark Antony!"

I was used to this kind of talk from Joe, even in Zack's

presence. I didn't think he could help himself. Unlike Melinda, I did not encourage it. I yawned and stretched and got up from the couch, remarking on how tired I was.

Joe stood up, too. "Are you sure you don't want another glass of wine?" he asked.

"Not a good idea. My head is swirling."

As I started walking, my knees buckled a little bit and I stumbled, but Joe was on hand to help me. He was so close, I felt his breath on my cheek. His clothes smelled of Clive Christian cologne. He continued to hold my waist even after I was steady. I gently but firmly removed myself from his embrace, said a hurried good night, and retreated to my room.

The way he touched me made me understand why women ended up in his bed. Swirling thoughts, but I eventually nodded off.

I am not sure what woke me up; I sat up and felt around for my cell phone. Two missed calls from Zack and one from Melinda. I would call them in the morning, I thought as I put the phone back on the table. It was well after midnight.

I lay back down and was about to succumb to sleep when I heard movement downstairs. Then some whispering. I smiled at the thought that even so late in the night, Joe was talking to some girl, most likely persuading her to come share the bed I had declined. The phone conversation, though inaudible, was interfering with my sleep, so I got up to close the door completely. Bits and pieces reached me.

"Yes, you guys are being careless. If that information gets out, we will lose the . . . I will do the best I can to calm things down . . . I will talk to her tomorrow, but you guys are messing up . . . we need her . . . yes . . ."

Could he be talking about me? I wondered. I edged forward.

"It seems . . . on to some lead, she's narrowing down on . . . we have to stop her."

It dawned on me how naive I had been. What was I thinking? Joe was Mark's friend. The reference to Mark under the guise of Antony. I should have understood the hint, the Freudian slip. No wonder he had been defending Mark for the past two days. And what did he mean by "we have to stop her"?

I did not wait to hear the rest. The one person I had always counted on for help was now my enemy. Part of the "they" Ben had alluded to.

I dressed and grabbed my handbag and the duffel bag with Kobi's games. I slid the cell phone into my jeans pocket and waited. I must have waited about an hour after Joe was done with the phone call. Now I had to make sure he was asleep. I tiptoed across the hall to Kobi's room and put my hand over his mouth and woke him up. "Sshhh," I whispered.

He looked confused but remained quiet. Carrying him, I tiptoed down the stairs past the lounge, through the kitchen, to the garage. I put Kobi in the backseat of the car and asked him to put on his seat belt. I jumped into the driver's seat and fumbled in my purse for the keys. I was shaking uncontrollably. After what seemed like a lifetime, I found them. I started the car, and as I began to reverse, I remembered that the garage door locked itself automatically at night. I had no idea how to disable it.

I turned around, trying to figure out what to do, and saw Joe coming toward the car. His eyes looked bloodshot, or maybe it was the light bouncing off his red silk pajamas.

He was saying something, but I didn't stop to hear. I may have been naive, but I was no fool. I locked the car right before he placed his hands on the door handle. Our eyes met for a split second. I read trouble. He seemed frustrated, almost desperate. I had never seen that look on his face.

"Mugure, it's okay, what are you doing?" he shouted, trying to soften his murderous look.

"Your schoolboy charm is not going to work on me again. Open the damn doors or I will drive through them," I shouted at him.

I did not wait for his response. I reversed the car and slammed it into the doors. They made a deafening sound but did not yield an inch. "Cover your ears, Kobi."

I had hoped that the loud bang would make Joe open the doors, out of fear of waking the neighbors, but he didn't. I engaged first gear and drove forward with force. Joe was out of sight. Where had he gone? If he had a gun, we were done for.

I looked to the side and saw him hunched over as if looking for something. I didn't wait to see what. I put the car in reverse, floored the gas pedal, and rammed into the garage doors. They gave a little but remained intact. I saw Joe approaching the car. I couldn't see if he was holding anything. He came running, waving, in front of the car. I narrowly missed him.

I put the car in reverse and stepped on the gas pedal again. I got a glimpse of Joe. What was he trying to do? I hit the doors again, and they gave a little more. One more time, I thought. Then Joe positioned himself in front of the car. He appeared to be holding something. I put the car in first and drove with such force that he had to escape by sprawling across the garage. I reversed once more and this time tore into pieces what was left of the garage door. The car swerved, but I managed to regain control and drive off. When I got to the road, I slowed down.

"We are safe now, we are safe," I said, looking in the rearview mirror. Kobi was not there. "Kobi?" I called out in a panic. I came to a screeching halt, unbuckled my seat belt, and looked in the back. I saw his little head sticking out. He had ducked under the seat. "It's okay to come out now, Kobi," I said.

A screeching sound made me look over my shoulder. The red sports car pulled up, almost touching mine. "Buckle up, Kobi, buckle up," I shouted, and sped off.

I floored the gas pedal. A light turned red in front of me. Joe was closing in. I ran the red light and turned right. I didn't see his car again until I was on the road leading to Interstate 95 South. My SUV was no match for his sports car, and before I knew it, he was tailing us. Then Joe moved into the left lane. We were parallel again. He rolled down his window, shouting inaudibles. The exit to New Rochelle was about two thousand feet away. I put the turn signal on. Joe scrambled to change lanes. I drove into the exit lane, Joe following. As soon as the road started to fork, I swerved the car left and got back on the highway as Joe sped off in the exit lane toward New Rochelle.

I kept driving till I reached the New York Palace Hotel on Madison Avenue and stopped right outside the entrance.

9

I managed to get Kobi to sleep at about two thirty in the morning. Only then did I allow myself to go over what had happened. Once again I thought of the hotline to Ben. A cautionary voice whispered the obvious: Something terrible had happened after I met with him. Yet what he had told me about the existence of a gang of "they" beat in my head like a drum. I called Zack. I felt tears of gratitude and relief when he answered.

"Why are you whispering? Is everything okay?" he asked.

"We just survived a car chase."

"A car chase? In a film?"

"No, running from Joe."

"What? Where are you? Where is Kobi?"

"We are fine. We just checked in to the Palace Hotel about an hour ago. But listen. Joe is working with Mark," I blurted out.

"Hold up, honey, what are you talking about?"

"Someone has been stalking me and sent me a surveillance video of myself. I was scared. I took refuge at Joe's. Then he tried to hurt us."

"What? Joe is a good guy, Mugure. I have known him for years. Are you really sure?"

"Are you doubting your wife? This has been the cause of our problems: You trust acquaintances, doubtful friends, strangers more than your wife."

"I'm sorry, Mugure," he said with a touch of pain. "But it's hard to imagine you and Joe in a car chase. That stuff happens in Hollywood."

"I'm not asking to you to imagine. This was not Hollywood."

"I know but, Mugure . . . Joe, why would he chase you? Look, I am sure there's an explanation for this."

"Zack!" I interrupted, "I haven't lost my mind."

"I am sorry. Listen very carefully. Do not go back to the house." He paused, then continued, "I need you to go to a place they cannot find you." I wasn't sure if he believed me or was just humoring me.

"Zack, do you think Joe is Mafia? He's Italian, you know," I started, but he interrupted me.

"Not every Italian is a member of the Mafia. My mother is the granddaughter of Italian immigrants, and she was not one. Besides what would the Mafia want from you?"

"You, Zack, you! Maybe they are after you and trying to get at you through me. Are you sure you have never been involved in shady business? Have you encountered the suited gunman?"

"Mugure, I can take care of myself. And please get this Mafia business out of your head. Otherwise, you will be seeing the Mafia in every Italian. I have not seen anybody following me. The gunman was bluffing."

I almost screamed. Ben told me that he'd seen the gunman board the same flight that Zack was on. Was Ben telling me a lie?

"Zack, you must learn to trust me, my judgment. I was right about Mark."

"Look, I don't know what to think right now. I am just worried about your safety. Why don't you guys get away from the tristate area? Go see our friends in California, or better yet, our friends in South Africa. Ciru. I can even join you there. A kind of holiday from all of this."

"A good idea. I mean, for you to join us. Sort things out away from these threats to your life. Our lives. I will see what's possible, but you are right, we need to get away."

We talked for a little while longer. He said he would put even more money into my account so that I could be flexible in my moves. Not that I needed it. He had been very generous with his money; he had set me up well.

"And, honey, I don't know if this will make you feel better, but I understand they let David out."

"David is out? That's good," I said. "What was he in for?"

"No charges. I don't know what they were after. I haven't talked to him."

Actually, the news made me feel better. I liked David. Still, I could not sleep: too many thoughts and feelings swirling in my head. Zack was right; I needed to get us as far away as possible, even from America. In this day of information technology, texting pics, there was not a state in the US where I could hide from those who were after my skull.

South Africa was looking good. Cape Town. Zack and I been there once. The hotels and cafés by the sea. The drive around Table Mountain. Oh yes, Kobi would love that. The view from the top. The air. So much to prepare for the journey. Buy tickets. And a little shopping. Not enough clothing. Shopping in New York or New Jersey? Mugure, you're crazy. Mafia. Joe. Mark. Get the hell out of here. Yawn. Sleep. Where could I go? There is Sam, my old flame. The man from Ohio . . . Ohio . . . Ohio . . .

Somehow I must have fallen asleep. I woke up early, as from a nightmare. Kobi was still asleep. Then my head began to clear. The events of yesterday. Ben. Joe. The chase. My talk with Zack. My thoughts. Sam. Ohio. I would go to Sam's place. What an inspiration. Neither Joe nor Mark knew Sam. I did not have his phone number. I immediately fired a message to Sam's Facebook page. I skipped the details, merely telling him that my child and I were in danger and we could use his help.

He replied later that morning. He would be more than glad to have us, he said. He included his phone number if I needed assurance. What a relief. But I could not help feeling a little guilt. I should not have neglected our friendship.

I then called my friend Ciru in Cape Town, saying we wanted to visit her for a couple weeks. She was excited. Now she was Dr. Ciru Mbai, assistant professor of sociology at the University of Cape Town. Seeing her would give me some fresh perspective. Zack would join us there; we would fly back to New York together, having calmly worked out a strategy.

By the time Kobi got up, I had settled on Ohio. We showered and went downstairs for breakfast in the hotel dining room. It was then that I felt the full impact of Joe turning foe.

The white male at the next table looked up from the newspaper he was reading, but as soon as our eyes met, he buried his head in the paper. The two men in business suits sitting not too far from him seemed to be looking our way constantly. The waiter came repeatedly to ask if we needed more coffee. Why? A couple stopped by our table and talked to Kobi. The man who kept passing by our table, pretending to be getting more breakfast, looked lean and mean. Every white man around me seemed to wear the face of a mafioso. I could feel their eyes on me. Maybe the stalker was capturing our every move on video.

As soon as Kobi and I checked out, we walked out to the street to hail a cab. I started waving cabs down, hoping to get one driven by a black or Asian man, preferably a woman. Black cabdrivers kept passing me by; the first cab that stopped was driven by a white man. I wasn't going to take chances, so I ignored it. Eventually, a turbaned Asian man stopped for us. I hesitated. Could he be a terrorist? I had become sensitive to men wearing beards and turbans. The thought of 9/11 brought to mind my conversation with Ben at the airport. How was the gunman connected with the scene of mass crime? Eventually, I chose a cab with a white woman driver. No woman had threatened my life yet, I reasoned.

I bought tickets for Ohio at LaGuardia Airport.

10

Sam and his father lived in a small quiet rural town outside of Cleveland. They were descended from some Swedish Finns who emigrated to America in the nineteenth century in the great Swedish migration to Minnesota and other parts of America, where they continued their Swedish-Finnish farming tradition.

I first met Sam when we were students at CCNY. He was rather shy, not voluble in social circles, and that was what drew me to him. He did not have strong views on many national or international matters except one: freeing America from slavery to foreign oil. He saw ethanol as the solution. I argued with him about it: Wouldn't it mean turning food into oil, taking away from humans and animals to feed cars? Yes, but one could grow enough to feed the human, the cow, and the car. He was taking business classes, but on his own, he followed the economics and politics of oil, at one time even paying his way to Brazil to study the industry. He was interested in developing a strain of corn with higher yields for ethanol.

He wanted me to move to Ohio, and for a moment I

was infatuated with the rural ideal, but I was dissuaded by one visit and the population of mostly older people who all seemed to dress in blue weather-beaten farm overalls. I suppose the Big Apple, its skyscrapers, yellow cabs, incessant honking, fever, yes, insomnia, had entered my system, and I could not see how I could endure the rural silence. Now, as a fugitive from eyes that watched me, I was looking for that peace and silence and some sleep.

Nothing had changed around the farm, or the area, for that matter. Not even the mailboxes on the road; they were the same color, apart from those whose paint had been washed out by the rain. I could not help admiring Sam for clinging to his passion and vision. It reminded me that I'd never had any strong passions, no vision to live for, fight for, or die for, if necessary.

His father sat in the yard wearing his eternal overalls. He must have just returned from the farm. As Kobi and I got out of the taxicab, he came up to us, and before I could figure out how to reintroduce myself, he called out: "Mugure! African queen!" I used to be so uncomfortable with that queen business when I was dating his son, but on this day, and after the ordeal I had gone through, it felt personal, welcoming. Sam joined us a couple of hours later, and as we sat on the porch munching roasted corn, I briefed them about my troubles. An edited version. No mention of suited gunmen.

After Kobi and Sam's father had turned in, Sam and I sat on the veranda. I lay down on the cushioned bench, and Sam sat on the wooden stairs, facing me.

"So when does Zack fly back in?" he asked.

"No firm plans. I'm thinking of flying to South Africa in a couple of days."

"Why travel all that way? You can stay right here with us."

"I don't want to burden you guys."

"You know I don't mind. You have always known that."

Yes, I did. He still liked me, it was obvious. The following day, as we took a tour around the farmhouse, I tinkered with the thought of staying in Ohio until Zack's return. I could busy myself as an extra hand on the farm. The more I thought about it, the better an option it seemed. Sam and I went for a walk and talked about everything except our past. Shopping for little things from the SouthPark Mall in Strongsville was a far cry from hectic Manhattan, but it was nice. Sometimes he would take Kobi to feed the pigs and cows. The cow became Kobi's favorite animal. It was nice to spend time with Sam and see him take to Kobi. It reminded me why we had dated in the first place.

One morning a day or two after I arrived, Sam's father called me in a conspiratorial voice. I followed him to the shed a few meters from the house. "Wait here a minute," he whispered.

He wasn't much of a talker except after the occasional glass of wine, which was always followed by a few war stories from Vietnam. Now he was sober, serious. He emerged from the shed with a shotgun hanging over his shoulder. "Ever held one of this?" he asked.

I thought of telling him about my brief experience at the shooting range in New York, when Okigbo had wanted to turn me into a cheaply paid security guard; about the gunman; or the gun at Zack's office. I didn't.

"No, I haven't, and I don't think I ever will," I said as

I followed him down the narrow path into the field till we came to a clearing.

"Listen, I am not going to let anybody hurt my African queen. I have been thinking about it. A car chase is not something you take to the police. No crime committed, they will say. But we have a right to defend ourselves. I am going to teach you how to deal with the bastards."

I was not sure I wanted to meddle with guns. I felt I had learned enough Krav Maga as protection, though it had not occurred to me that I could use my martial arts to defend Kobi and me. The instructors had taught us defense moves against a gun held at close quarters but not how to use one. Perhaps martial skills needed bolstering with smoking metal. Besides, there was nothing wrong with indulging the old man.

At first I felt silly, intimidated, by the feel of the gun in my hands. But my teacher was not giving up and encouraged me to fire. "The key is to aim. Aim, aim, and aim again. Your hands must be steady. Take a deep breath and pull the trigger. If someone is trying to kill, they will stop at nothing. Don't doubt it. So if you want to live another day, you shoot the son of a bitch first."

I fired. My first shot ever in my life. I felt blood rush through me, very close to how I sometimes felt about Krav Maga. I was surprised at my excitement and fired a few more times.

"Not bad for a first time," he said as he doubled over with laughter, "but enough for the day."

It became a daily routine. He was a gun lover and had all sorts of weapons. He let me practice with the different pistols. He insisted I practice to shoot with both hands and at different positions, standing, running, rolling on the ground. I was never going to be a crack shot, but I was grateful that he was making me take charge of my own security.

One afternoon when Kobi and Sam went to supervise the milking of the cows, I took a walk around the neighborhood. It was nice to have some quiet moments on my own in the streets of Ohio. Though the people worked extremely hard, they were a little laid-back, not fussy, but kind.

In a way, the place reminded me of rural Kenya. Even the smells of fresh air and farmland brought memories of the Kakuyu of my childhood. I remembered my mother tending her small herbal garden on a Saturday afternoon. Sometimes she would sit on the grass and knit, sometimes she would take an afternoon nap. Every time I saw her out in the garden, I would grab something to snack on and make myself comfortable in the shade. And every time she would go on about how I needed to learn how to knit or sew. I would divert the conversation to what had happened to me over the week or days or hours: how I saw a man with ears that looked like a rabbit's and I'd asked him where he got them; or how I was so curious about safari ants and put out my finger and got bitten; or how I had tricked a bully boy into running away by shouting to an imaginary mother, "Hurry up with the machete, Mom." She would warn me against acts that hurt others, but sometimes she would laugh so hard at my antics that tears flowed down her cheeks. She would pull herself straight and end up with "You are a crazy child." I missed her terribly and wished she were alive. I felt a need to connect with her. I wondered what she would say to my situation now. I knew she would not approve of the drinking. You have to let it go, she would have told me. It will cloud your better judgment. Yes, she would give me good advice, tell me I was a crazy child, but support me all the same.

Pity my mother was gone. And a shame that my father, though alive, was not really in my life. I liked Sam's relationship with his dad; theirs was a love with mutual respect. Sam's dad was not into the ethanol business: Farming for him was cows, pigs, and fruit orchards. But he supported his son's dreams. Why had I been denied such a relationship? Why hadn't my father wanted me? I did not know anything about him, his family, his life. I wondered how it must have felt for him to let me grow up without ever seeing me, touching me, washing my tears, admonishing me, saying to me: You have done well, my daughter. I guessed I would never know who he was, what really made him tick, why he made the choices he had made. I would never find out. Unless I paid him a visit. Could I really face him after our last and only meeting? What if he asked about the white boys he had warned me against? I wondered. But I was a grown-up. I didn't need anything from him. I could ask him questions directly. For far too long, I had avoided attempts to find answers to my questions. It was as if I did not want to confront Kenya, my past, my Africanness, my blackness. Perhaps Ben had been right.

As I walked back to the house, I realized I had been gone for over an hour. I was tired from the walk, but I had talked myself into visiting my father. It would be a personal journey, my journey. I would go to Kenya for a few days of talk with my father, and touch base with Wainaina and Jane, and then come back. There was the unfinished quest for the Kenya counterpart of the Kasla agency. Call it curiosity or obstinacy, but the more I thought about the idea, the better it sounded. That evening I started making arrangements.

I had told Zack that I was staying in Ohio with an old college friend while I organized the trip to Cape Town. I continued to let Zack believe Kobi and I would be heading there. The many unanswered questions had eroded my trust in Zack, though not to where I could let go of him. What if I were wrong? The on-and-off attitudes; the doubt and the will to believe; the repulsion and the attraction: It was a mini-war in me. But even if I were in harmony with self, as before, I knew that the Kenya trip had to be mine alone. Maybe after I came back from Kenya and he from Estonia, we could travel to Cape Town as a family. I would be a new Mugure, at ease with her past and secure in the results of her quest for the roots of the threats to our lives.

With that, I bought a return ticket to Kenya using my credit card. Sam agreed to keep Kobi until I returned, which I hoped would not be over a week. I knew Kobi would be safe here, perhaps even like it. I did not want to add to their already hectic daily routines, so I turned to Rosie. She had few objections to coming to Ohio. It was not a bad move for her financially.

I was sad to part with Kobi. But in some strange way, I felt it was necessary; that the future I would give him depended on how honestly I could confront my past. Or rather, his past and mine were tied in a common knot of mystery, and the key to the mystery lay in Kenya.

Part Two

11

I was born out of an affair between my mother, a school dropout, and an older person who offered support on the condition that she did not publicly proclaim him the father. She paid for the silence: Her brother, with whom she had lived since the death of their parents, kicked her out in the street.

My father bought her a stone house in Kakuyu, near Nairobi. It was known as the uniform hub because nurses, policemen, security personnel, and drivers—all in the uniforms of their trade—lived there. Our house was near a road whose tar had largely worn off, and during the rainy season, cars got stuck in the mud. The drivers and their assistants would scatter rocks and gravel under the tires for traction. Sometimes they would ask us, the children, or any onlookers to help rock the cars back and forth, and we would end up with mud all over our clothes. Quite often they would bring a bigger vehicle to tow the one stuck. The noise level was unbearable. The area made up for its run-down appearance with its location, fifteen minutes from the city center.

I can't remember my father ever coming to the place. I never found out how much he gave my mother or how it was done. I just knew that he paid for my education and gave us enough to keep us from starving. My mother supplemented the income by taking poorly paid cleaning jobs at the offices of the Ministry of Health and Sanitation. She also planted kale, tomatoes, rosemary, basil, and thyme, some of which she sold to the local kiosks. No matter how exhausted, she would make sure to visit her garden, pull out a weed or two, or simply smell the rosemary. It was her personal ritual, and she would come out of it seemingly refreshed.

Long-legged and dark-skinned, with big brown eyes set slightly above her round cheekbones in almost perfect symmetry, my mother always walked with her back straight, believing that slouching bent one's body and spirit. Her wide sunny smile thrilled me. She liked singing and was part of the Kakuyu Church women's choir. She never married—I don't know whether out of love of independence or some kind of loyalty to my father—and she didn't have more children. Sometimes I would catch her off guard with a distant look in her eyes. She appeared so lonely, and that made me sad, but as soon as she became aware of my presence, she would light up, dispelling my sadness.

Only once did my father express interest in meeting with me. My mother had told him that I was accepted at City College of New York, and he asked that I collect the plane ticket from him in person. I begged her to tell me more about him and their relationship to prepare me for the encounter. Other than his name—George Gata, or GG, as my mother referred to him—I didn't know much else. She smiled enigmatically.

My father lived alone but had similar pacts with other women with whom he had sired children: support on condition that they did not tarnish his image as an eternal bachelor, a *muthuri mwanake,* or bachelor polygamist, as my mother put it in Gikuyu. She painted a portrait of a decent man whose only shortcoming was that he had denied himself the wealth that comes from contact with children. She didn't like it when I said that he was a mean bastard for denying me a father. She defended him as a good and generous man who did not know how to express love. Did she know the other woman or women? I asked her. No. Did she know the other children? No.

"You see, a dog in the manger," I countered. "He has no right to deny me my sisters and brothers by hiding us from each other." My mother was not too pleased to hear my view. To mollify her, I added quickly that I was curious and looked forward to the meeting. My sudden conversion from indifference to eagerness alarmed her.

"Please, Mugure, watch your tongue. He is a good man," she pleaded.

Well, the good man kept me waiting in the lobby of his office. I looked around the room, trying to figure out what sort of business he ran. On the walls hung several calendars and pictures of long-haul trucks. The exercise irritated and agitated me: I should not have to guess that my own father was in the transportation business. Over the years, I had reconciled with not having a father, and I didn't want this peace broken. I rushed to the bathroom to empty my bladder.

When I was finally invited in, I found the good man standing at the corner of the office with the demeanor of a person waiting for a bus due any minute. He was bald with a potbelly, the roundest I had ever seen, that seemed to rise up to meet his chest with every breath. No matter how hard I tried, I could not see the eternal lover in his figure. How could my mother have fallen in love with this man? Was it even love? I wondered.

"A spitting image of your mother," he said almost to himself, and continued staring at me as if looking for a trace of himself. "How did you get that?" he asked, pointing at my ear. "Remarkable. Same birthmark as my father, in the exact same spot." He chuckled and then muttered almost to himself, "The son of a bitch."

I felt like throwing the words back at him for keeping me standing, but he finally asked me to sit down. When growing up, I used to picture our meeting quite differently. In my dream encounter, he hugged me at once and assured me that he was going to forge a new father/daughter relationship to make up for all the missing years. He would introduce me to my siblings, and we would live happily ever after. Reality was rude, this one at least. I started to say something unflattering, then stopped and shifted my gaze. His office furniture was made of exotic wood inlays and burls covered with pure leather. It exuded power and success.

"So, what are you going to study?" he asked, coming to the reason for my visit.

"Education, but I haven't really—"

"All the way to America to train as a teacher? You could do it right here, and it would not cost me so damn much."

For the sake of my mother, I looked away again to avoid saying something rude.

"America is a very expensive place," he was saying. "Two of my daughters are studying there. I tell you what. I will offer you the same deal. I will pay for your tuition and upkeep for four years. After that, you are on your own. Do you understand?"

I wanted to ask him about those daughters, my siblings, their names, their ages, and where they studied. They must be older, so did I have younger sisters? Brothers? Where? Did they have the same birthmark? Then I remembered my mother's plea to remain polite and simply said thank you.

At the door, with the check for my ticket in my hands, I glanced over my shoulder, but he had already gone back to reading the pile of papers on his desk. His voice reached me outside: "Watch out for those white boys. They like beautiful African women."

My mother died in an accident two years after I left Kenya—she was hit by a tow truck on the road outside her house. The good man was my only parent, and until now I had not made any efforts to get in touch with him, let alone get to know him. It was ironic that I was flying home to tell him that I had a white boy for a husband.

Only I did not know which face of Zack's whiteness I would present: the loving owner of a bellyful of laughter, a senior attorney at Edward and Palmer, or a secretive lying lawyer living under the shadow of my suspicions and that of a mysterious gunman.

12

When I finally found myself outside the Jomo Kenyatta airport after a grueling fifteen-hour review of my life, I stopped, closed my eyes, and took in the sweet smell of home. The breeze. The freshness.

Wainaina walked toward me, his smile sending out a sunny embrace. "The man with a body to die for," I said as I hugged him, to remove any lingering embarrassment about my outburst at New York University years ago.

"Yours is no less killing," he said. "Good to see you, Mugure. You haven't changed."

"Neither have you. Nairobi, perhaps."

"The skyline, yes, otherwise not much. I have been sitting in traffic for two hours."

I was about to say it was like that when I was here for my honeymoon when I recalled that we never actually came to Nairobi. The extension of our honeymoon from Estonia to Kenya had been my idea. Zack had thought Estonia was enough, especially since I had taken to the old town so intensely, but I insisted out of a sense of equity and pride. Zack had told me that he'd never been to

Kenya, and I thought of it as my contribution to the honeymoon bliss. With the help of my friend Jane, I picked out the best resorts in Malindi and Mombasa, with their amazing views of the endlessly blue waters of the Indian Ocean. I also planned trips to Maasai Mara and to the Treetops Hotel in Nyeri, but a week before we were to leave, Zack got an urgent message requesting his return to New York.

"I avoided Narobi traffic by confining my honeymoon to the coast," I said. "I missed you, though."

"You mean you avoided me?"

"I did not want my flame to dim when set against you," I said.

"His name?"

"Zack Sivonen. And you? Are you hooked up with somebody, or should I divorce Zack?"

"Still a bachelor. But no divorcée for me."

I loved our banter. It assumed a friendly familiarity but also a respectful distance. He took my suitcase, and we walked to a nearby taxi. I gave Jane's home address to the driver. As we drove farther on Mombasa Road, the vehicles moved at a snail's pace all the way to James Gichuru Road. Peddlers welcomed the traffic; they walked beside the cars, trying to sell their wares, pens, watches, cell phones, calling cards, newspapers, anything they could hold in their hands.

Bright-colored public minibuses tried to overcome the jam by driving on the shoulder, sending scores of cyclists and pedestrians scampering for safety on the side of the road or right into the thorny, spiny shrub around apartment blocks.

"The speed limit is generally viewed as the government's conspiracy to slow down their business," Wainaina said. "*Matatu* drivers ignore it all the time. Even the traffic lights are taken as decoration."

I was going to stay with Jane. She had offered me her place, saying she would be offended if I stayed in a hotel. "Your husband refused to let you come here on your honeymoon," she had joked on the phone. "Time for girl talk, you and I, without sons and husbands."

Jane had never married and did not want any children, and over time, her relatives and friends alike had come to terms with the fact. She had held her views on children and marriage for as long as I could remember, even in high school. Knowing her as a rabble-rouser who was involved in every student crisis, I would not have seen her getting into law school, let alone graduating with honors from Harvard.

And now here she was, one of the most successful attorneys in Kenya, working with Lawson, Anderson, and Wilson. It was one of the oldest firms in the country, founded in the early years of the colony. Before and up to independence, it was solely European, but after, while retaining the same name and reputation, it had taken in African and Asian partners. The owners had wanted the firm known by its initials, LAW, but they were satisfied with the more popular initials SOL, for Sons of Law. She still volunteered her services at the Federation of Women Lawyers (FIDA). She took her work seriously but played hard on weekends, so I would not be an intrusion. At least so I hoped.

She came out of her Lavington house to welcome us to her place.

"Meet the man with a body to die for," I announced, introducing Wainaina.

"Or a body to live for," Jane said, casting a wicked glint at me.

I knew what it meant. "I am happily married, and he just told me he's not interested in a divorcée. Jane has always been a troublemaker, you know," I told Wainaina, then quickly explained, to Jane's raucous laughter, how the phrase came to be.

"She made all the women in New York avoid me. Nobody wanted to die," Wainaina said. He looked shy or embarrassed as he stretched his hand out to Jane. It turned out they knew each other by name, she as the sharp-tongued lawyer from SOL, and he as the nationally known investigative journalist with the *Daily Star*. "He's the shining star of the newspaper world," Jane said, to which Wainaina responded with appreciative modesty: "Thank you, I'll take it coming from you."

A warm shower and a change of clothes made me feel fresh and relaxed. Soon we were tearing into baked chicken served with soup and peas, corn, and mashed potatoes. The food brought back happy memories.

"I'm here for a week," I told them. "I want to do in seven days what I have not done all my life."

I talked in detail about what I had experienced in the past few weeks. Hopefully, I said, my pursuers would lose the trail. They sat there, transfixed.

"So where would you like to start?" Jane asked me.

"I really don't know. Obviously, with my father. A daughter with a thousand questions and a father with a thousand secrets. Suppose we start with those matters where I most need your help? I want to find the local adoption agency and sort out the contradictory information about Kobi. If we can do that this afternoon, then tomorrow I can visit with my father. The Mafia connection will be made clear by what we find about the links between Nairobi and New York."

"That's a good starting point. After all, your problems began with your visit to that Kasla place," Jane said.

"By the way," Wainaina interjected, "I was able to get some more information about the agencies that didn't respond to your messages. The one in Westlands is owned by a woman by the name of Maryanne Stanley. She's Kenyan, but I suppose the name Stanley sounds more professional. I don't know why people do these things; I am happy with Wainaina. But she's a really nice person. Her agency only deals with orphaned children; they don't work directly with any particular agency outside the country. It was closed down for renovation, but it's back in business. That leaves us with Three Ms. As I told you, I found their logo interesting."

"Who owns it?" I asked.

"I'm coming to that. First the name. Three Ms: Miwani Miracle Ministries. The logo is just a graphic representation of the Swahili word Miwani, or glasses, hence vision. Clever, isn't it?"

"An interesting evolution. Ever since I lost the case of the Alternative Clinics—" Jane began.

"Oh, you are the Jane of the alternative clinics," Wainaina interrupted. "The *Daily Star* covered the case, but they called you Mr. Kagendo. The guy who captioned it was given a verbal thrashing by the editor. That's how I came to be in charge of copyediting as well."

"You mean you have to thank me for your promotion," Jane said.

"You might say so."

"I want my cut, then."

"You mean a pound of flesh?" I asked. I could not help it. *The Merchant of Venice* was one of the Shakespeare plays staged at Msongari in my time, and I thought Jane played Portia to my Shylock.

"'The quality of mercy is never strained,'" Wainaina said, casting a glance at Jane.

"'It droppeth as the gentle rain from heaven / Upon the place beneath; it's twice blest,'" Jane said, and looked at me.

"'It blesseth him that gives and him that takes,'" I intoned, not to be outdone.

We were beside ourselves with laughter. Bantering had quickly become our way.

"Come to think of it, your interest in law may have started with your playing the amateur lawyer," I said to Jane.

"Probably. Jokes aside," Jane continued, "losing the case dampened my spirits. But I believe this 3M business may have started under the name the Real Alternative Clinics. Almost like— I would not call it gloating, but definitely piggybacking on the earlier name, or the loss of it."

The affair seemed to have impacted my friend profoundly, but I did not want to lose the trail. "So who owns Three Ms?"

"Susan, I think, a reverend."

"The one Susan?" Jane asked.

"Susan, Her Holy Reverend, or officially Her Holiness, but she uses the titles interchangeably. Jane, you must know her?" Wainaina said.

"I don't, but which Kenyan does not know of her?" Jane said.

Her Holy Reverend, the leader and founder of Miwani Miracle Ministries and founder and owner of Three Ms, aka the Real Alternative Clinics, emerged as a boisterous, robust, slightly overweight, and charismatic woman and skilled orator.

"You have to give it to her," said Jane. "That is, if we are talking about the same Susan. Her meteoric rise to the top echelon in the society, with connections to every center of power, from Parliament to the army, police, and political parties, is astounding by any standards. At national events, she is often called upon to bless the nation."

"The more data I gathered about her," Wainaina resumed his narrative, "the more I found myself admiring her. My research gave me a little window into her character and dynamic personality . . ."

She was brilliant enough to have been admitted to the prestigious Alliance High School, but her father could not afford the tuition. She landed a job as a filing clerk in the Ministry of Education, but with six brothers and sisters who all relied on her meager salary, she found life pretty difficult, and it was then, in the depth of misery and sorrow, that she had her first call from Jesus. She became a devout Christian. Those who recalled her days as a youth member of the Ngarariga church said she was an extremely resourceful organizer of fund-raising events.

It was then, so the story goes, that she introduced the idea of a church-run raffle for the benefit of the poorer congregation. The winner would earn two plane tickets to Mombasa. Susan chaired a small committee that handled the raffle tickets. She involved the whole congregation in prayer that the ticket should go to the chosen one. When it turned out that the chosen one was one of her brothers, some irate congregates objected and accused her of naked nepotism. Deeply upset that they should question the mysterious ways of God, Susan quit the church and went into the wilderness. For a year nobody knew her whereabouts. Then she emerged from wherever she had been, literally in rags, with scratches on her arms that she claimed came from wrestling with satanic cactus thorns in the wilderness. She told a harrowing, heart-wrenching story of how, in the depths of her tribulations, sorrow, and despair, the Lord visited her in the form of a bird and said: "Susan, rise, follow me, and I shall make you fishers of men." A born-again Christian, she founded her own church under a tree in Limuru and told the story of her call over and over again, asking the congregation, "Have you ever heard a bird speak?" The Holy Spirit assumed the body of a bird and spoke to her.

Within a few years she had moved from a tree to a rented classroom and then her own church building, where she led the hymn: "Count your blessings, count them one by one, and you will see what the Lord has done for you." They flocked to her church to count their blessings, making sure they brought their tithes. Miwani became the fastest-growing church in the country, and its branches could be found in most cities across the country. In honor of the tree under which her church was founded, every branch planted a tree, which was blessed by Reverend Susan.

"How did she acquire the title 'Her Holiness'?" I asked, fascinated.

"That's another story," Wainaina said. "If you go to

her church, as I had to do several times, the first thing you will notice is the mixture of Roman Catholic and High Anglican rituals, a far cry from the puritanism of the beginnings, when her church was characterized by bareness, simplicity. Wherever she goes—and there came a time when she started traveling beyond our borders—she would add another ritual and claim it had been revealed to her by God. This is what she did when she returned from some Eastern European countries, Estonia or Latvia, and brought rituals of the Orthodox Church. Her church now is a Kenyan version of the Santería in Cuba. And each time she comes back from her travels, she makes incredible claims: It was after she returned from the East that she proclaimed she was responsible for the fall of godless communism. Never mind that her visit was several years after the fall of the Berlin Wall and the collapse of the Soviet system . . . You asked me how she became Her Holiness. Susan visited the US, and when she came back, she said she had met a Black Angel."

"Literally?" Jane asked.

"Literally. At least so her followers believe. Sometimes they talk of a choir of black angels. And when they talk about it, they burst into song, a call-and-response version of 'Swing Low, Sweet Chariot.'

> *I looked over Jordan, and what did I see*
> *Coming for to carry me home*
> *A band of angels coming after me*
> *Coming for to carry me home.*

"Her followers believe she did not fly back to the country in a regular plane. A band of angels carried her shoulder-high all the way from America across the Atlantic to Africa—"

"What's wrong, Mugure?" Jane and Wainaina asked in unison.

It was nothing, really. It was the audacity of the coincidence. I told them about the three incidents involving encounters with a Susan-type woman: Estonia, with Zack; and Melinda, in New York.

"Religion has become the fastest-growing industry in the country," Jane added.

"I don't blame her. All over the world, religion means money. The Vatican, after all, is richer than many countries in the world," said Wainaina.

"But you must give Susan some credit," chimed in Jane. "She is quite shrewd. Hundreds of businesses are owned by her or linked to her. Beauty salons, dry cleaners, makeshift small hotels, import/export, anything. She does not thrive by faith alone."

"Yes, but she puts faith in every business," said Wainaina. "Remember the name of her church: Miwani Miracle Ministries. She believes in angels and miracles, and hers are not abstract. You might think, for instance, that the curios in her shops are ordinary. No, no. She has breathed into them the breath of the black angel."

"Curios? How do you mean?" I asked, the name ringing a thousand bells in my mind.

"Yes, she owns curio shops all over. Apparently, they have tried to export abroad, directly or with partners, but not everybody in Europe and the US is as gullible as we Kenyans when it comes to faith. Her followers believe that those giraffes and elephants and Maasai warriors can transmit the breath of angels to the owner."

I told them about the Rhino Man of the Manhattan curio shop.

"Reverend Susan is an interesting character," Jane said, "but I doubt she would let herself get involved in murky business. Why would she do in the dark what she can do for profit in the light?"

"Yes, she profits by the light," Wainaina said. "There is the Festival of Rags, for instance."

"Festival of Rags?" I said, more as a statement than a question. Melinda had mentioned it at the end of her season at Shamrock, the same night we were confronted by the suited gunman.

"That's right. Starting from nothing, her church grew; her own blessings grew; her money multiplied; her garments became increasingly expensive. She founded the festival to celebrate her rise from rags to riches and remind her followers of the humble beginnings. This year's star performer is a woman advertised as having the voice of an angel. There are a few posters in town to that effect," Wainaina said.

"Her name is Melinda," I said. "She's my friend. She does possess a golden voice. She isn't aware yet that I am in Kenya."

I did not know if Melinda and Zack were in touch, but I didn't want her to leak my presence in the country. Ciru Mbai and I had agreed that should Zack or anybody else call about me, she would act as if Kobi and I were her guests in Cape Town. I had said the same to Sam and the folk in Ohio: To every inquiry, South Africa was the answer.

Melinda's imminent arrival settled the order of business; we had to see Susan before she did. Wainaina would wear his colors as a journalist. I would have liked to get on with it right away, but we had talked into the night, and jet lag was catching up with me.

Jane offered Wainaina a place to crash. I bade them good night and walked to my bedroom. Fatigued in mind and body, I slept without dreams of gunmen, car chases, or the Mafia.

13

I called Ohio first thing in the morning to say I had arrived safely and to check on Kobi. My son had gone to bed, Sam told me. Rosie was taking good care of him. A remarkable woman, Sam said of her, and assured me there was nothing to worry about. I detected slight stress in his voice. There was something he wasn't telling me.

"Is everything okay?" I asked him, a little alarmed. It was nothing much, he assured me, just a man who claimed to be a police officer. Ben was his name. I held my breath. Had it anything to do with Zack and the suited gunman? A fatal gunfight in Tallinn? It was nothing to worry about, Sam said again, Ben had called to speak to me.

"When I told him I did not know how to reach you, he called me by name. I was surprised he knew we used to date. He said you had been on the run, and he had reason to believe that I was hiding you, and I would be held responsible should anything happen to you. Mugure, you understand, I don't want trouble with the police. I admitted you had been here but that you had left for South Africa. I gave him Ciru's contact in Cape Town."

"How the hell did Ben trace me to you?" I wondered.

"Traffic lights, cameras, and Joe. Mugure, you ran several red lights on your way to and from Joe's. He's actually the one who called Ben. Joe claimed you were crazy and urged the police to commit you to psychiatric observation. I assured him that you seemed quite sane to me, and I told him about Joe trying to hit you. Joe is under their umbrella of suspicion, Ben said, though he did not elaborate. He said you should call, that I must tell you to get in touch with him. He talked of a hotline. Please call him."

I looked at my phone after we were done. The missed calls confirmed Sam's story: Ben had tried to get in touch with me. I did not know what made me angrier, Ben hinting that I was on the run, or Joe covering his murderous deeds by claiming I was mentally deranged. No, I was not about to call Ben. I had a little work to do.

The drama from Ohio was on my mind when I set out for the Miracle Church with Wainaina at the wheel of Jane's car. I had to fake a cheerfulness I did not feel. He had already reported for work, talked to his editor about a possible story on the Festival of Rags, and been given the go-ahead. That meant he would work with me the entire day. Jane excused herself, wishing us good luck rather skeptically. She said she would help whenever her schedule allowed.

We had worked out an angle. Wainaina was the lead journalist and I his cameraperson, intending to do several stories on MMM leading up to the Festival of Rags. Beginning with the Three Ms agency, we would follow the story of adoptees from Kenya to their adopted homes and families abroad. We hoped she would show us written records and answer questions. The process of elimination would surely lead us to the Kasla partner agency.

The building was surrounded by a stone wall, with broken pieces of glass firmly cemented on top to discourage anyone from climbing over. We stopped by the blue metal gates.

The security guard peered at us through the small hole in the gate before stepping out. Wainaina took out his press card and explained our mission, an interview with Susan. The man looked at the ID, returned it, and said that Reverend Susan had already left and would not be back until evening prayers. In any case, we could not see her without an appointment. Could we see the church? No, the premises were open to the public during the hours of worship only, but we could look at the building from outside the gate without taking pictures.

Wainaina parked the car on the side. I had expected lots of activity, with cars and people going in and out of the church compound. "For some reason, I thought the church was located in the city center," I said to Wainaina.

"This has been here all the time," the man said. "After the holy tree, the Holy Spirit guided her here."

"How long have you worked here?" Wainaina asked.

"Do I sound like I don't know what I am saying?" replied the watchman, turning hostile.

"No, no, my brother here means no harm. He just wants to ask a few questions, since we can't see the reverend," I said, and looked in my bag.

"Then teach him. You seem to have more sense," he said, eyeing the movement of my hands.

Wainaina got the hint and brandished a thousand-shilling

note. The watchman looked around, beady-eyed, and motioned toward the money. "Young man, this is not enough to buy a beer. The Americans who come here, they pay more, even if they are asking me where's the madam!"

I dug in my purse and took out a ten-dollar bill.

"You American?" he asked.

I shook my head. "Been traveling," I said vaguely, and quickly added, "We wanted to know a little bit about the history of the church."

"Good people. You have shown a lot of sense. I wish I could help you with the past. But I cannot tell you a lie. Even Americans who come and ask, I tell them the truth. I was not here from the beginning. I know some who were here. But they have left. I don't know how or why."

At first he mentioned Magda, his neighbor at Kaloleni; as he did not have her number, he gave us directions to her house. Then he remembered Kivete Kitete, who also lived in Kaloleni but was easier to reach, because he was a regular at the bar Memories, in Dagoretti, a few minutes away.

"Does everyone who works here live in Kaloleni?" an amused Wainaina asked.

"If you want to know about the present," the guard continued, igoring Wainaina, "I'm your man."

"Tell us, what happens here?" I asked out of curiosity.

"Miracles. My brother and sister, I have seen the blind see, the deaf hear, the lame walk, and the possessed become whole again. Once some demons the reverend had cast out of some sinners came running, felled me with invisible blows, and by the time I got to my feet, they had opened the gate and gone. Down the road, they entered some donkeys who started hee-hawing in unison—"

"What's your name?" Wainaina interrupted the flow.

"Kamau," he said.

"We shall come again to hear the rest," Wainaina said, and handed him some money.

"Whenever you come, day or night, ask for me, your friend Kamau."

Memories was located in what seemed like a vast chicken yard. The chickens crisscrossed the road as often as the humans, narrowly avoiding the speeding cars. They ate from the open sewage a cocktail of paper, plastic, fruits, goat pee, and human shit; the stink hit my nostrils with a vengeance. The daily market had folded up. Only a few people remained, selling small packets of cooking oil, onions, curry powder, and love potions, potent aphrodisiacs, some told Wainaina, casting meaningful glances at me.

Kenny Rogers's "The Gambler" was blasting from the high-pitched speakers meant to tell those outside that Memories was bursting with life. The stench of beer and hot air hit me and made me retreat a step before gathering courage to proceed. The many unoccupied tables—each with four wooden chairs, an ashtray, and a menu on top—made the bar appear emptier than it really was. The clients were boisterous enough to give the impression of a crowded place. We chose a table on the left side of the bar. Soon a lean woman in her midthirties, wearing a short skirt and a white top with MEMORIES written in small print, was at our table.

"How are you today? My name is Martha," she said with a smile. "Can I get you some drinks before you order food? We have the best roasted goat meat in the world. Can I bring you a few pieces? Tasting only?"

We ordered a kilo of *nyama choma* with boiled potatoes. Wainaina ordered a Tusker beer, and I requested a
soda. I asked her if she knew Kivete.

"Kivete, your fame precedes you," she said in the direction of a group of men sitting at one of the tables. "Visitors
to see you."

"Visitors? I am coming," a man shouted back, grab-
bing his beer and walking toward us. He was tall, dressed
in a khaki shirt and pants. He took two puffs of the cigarette that dangled from his mouth and exhaled a large
cloud of smoke that hid his gray hair and beard for a
second or two.

"I am Kivete Kitete," he said as he shook my hand, then
Wainaina's, before crushing the stub of a cigarette in the
ashtray.

I offered him a beer, which he accepted readily, shouting to Martha to bring him a cold one.

"So how can I help you?" he asked me.

"We understand you worked for Reverend Susan?"

"Who told you that?"

"We just heard—"

"I bet it was that useless security guard at the gate.
Kamau talks too much. He keeps the gates shut, but his
mouth . . . aii! You ask for one bean and he spills all, inter-
spersing every remark with 'American this, American that,'
you would think Americans come to see him daily. But I
am not like that, it's hard to get me to talk." He stopped
abruptly, sprang to his feet, and started dancing. "This is
my favorite Kamaru song," he said, and sang out loud: "*Ni
nyuo ni nyuo ni ya mwana, ni nyuo ni nyuo.*"

Kivete shook his lean body like someone on crystal
meth. Martha joined in the dancing. Then all the other

clients moved to the center and formed a circle of dancing feet. Wainaina sang along, nodding to the beat. I was wondering if I should not take the initiative and ask him to dance when Kivete rushed back and, before I could tell what he was doing, took my hand and dragged me to the dance floor, which prompted Wainaina to jump to the floor in a protective gesture. Soon we were all swaying this way and that, singing louder than the jukebox. It was over as fast as it had started. I walked back to our table, followed closely by Kivete and Wainaina.

"I used to be the best dancer back in the day." Kivete chattered on about how all the girls would chant his name over and over again. "Martha, give me another beer," he shouted, though he had barely sipped the other one. "And give the bill to my new friends here."

"So why did you stop working for Reverend Susan?" I tried again.

"Ah, Reverend Susan . . . She was breathing down my neck. Never let me do my job. 'Do this, Kivete, do that, Kivete.'"

"What work?" I asked.

"I was the director of appearance."

"What did your job entail?" I asked, wondering if he was attempting humor.

"Making sure the church looked good at all times."

"Cleaning?"

"Yes. Not just any cleaning, the professional kind. But she didn't respect my work, saying I was always coming late."

"What happened?" Wainaina asked.

"I quit."

"Does she run the business entirely by herself?" Wainaina tried. "Does she work with other people? Other companies?"

"It's hard to say, but I never thought that was her church, you know. It was as if she were standing in for some big shot in government. There's that minister of faith and religion, Kaguta. A regular at her church. These men are clever; they get a woman to front for them. Politics in this country, my friend, are difficult to understand. But I tell you what, the Festival of Rags is coming. Sometime this week. You can learn more from the goings-on in the festival than from any interview with me or Kamau."

It was impossible to get anything more specific from Kivete. The beer did not help. Was it his strategy and tactic? Talk without saying anything? As we stood up to go, I thought I would give it one more shot. "Kivete, tell me, please, what did you mean by director of appearance? Cleaning? That stuff that needed professional care?"

I thought I saw Kivete look over his shoulder; I had seen the same gesture in Kamau. But while Kamau still worked there, Kivete had already left, so why? For a second he seemed sober. He came closer and talked to me in a low voice, as if he did not want Wainaina to hear.

"Some people become a nuisance. They run off at the mouth. Say they have been close to her. They have seen things. Do you think she will let anybody bring down what she has built? She is the judge. There have to be cleaners. I was fired when I said no. My sister, I like you." The focus shifted to me. "The way you danced, be careful, and I mean very careful."

I felt a chill. Did he mean what I thought he meant? I wasn't sure if I could take Kivete seriously. Wainaina didn't, when I told him what the man had told me. "Kivete is too dramatic for me," Wainaina said. He hoped Magda would be less drama and provide more information.

It was early afternoon. We set out for Kaloleni.

We parked the car by the road near a Bell Properties sign and walked down a narrow path for a couple of yards before we saw the brown stone house we had been told to look out for. The path to the door passed through a small potato garden directly in front. The door was opened by an elderly woman in a flowery dress with a shawl wrapped around her shoulders and a head scarf with a blue cross that meant she was part of a women's church guild.

"Good afternoon. My name is Mugure. This is my friend Wainaina. We are looking for Magda?"

"What do you want from her?" the woman asked as she looked us over.

"Oh, we are friends of her old workmates."

She looked at us suspiciously and, without moving her eyes, called out, "Magda, your workmates are here."

A woman of medium height peered around her mother's elbows. "I don't know who these people are, Mother," she said, looking at us.

The standoff was becoming embarrassing. Just then a hen came flying from behind the house, clucking loudly. Behind the hen was a dog eager to have chicken for an afternoon snack. I immediately sprang into action and managed to catch the poor hen right before the dog did. I handed it over to Magda's mother. She took the bird and threatened the dog with violence. "I don't know who leaves the door open. This dog will eat up all the chicken," the woman said to us, grateful that I had saved the hen from early demise. She asked Magda to let us in and make us some tea.

We sat on red couches; red flowers embellished the coffee tables, covered with white cloths with red patterns. Magda walked in holding a red flask and some mugs with big red hearts. She was wearing a military fatigue shirt over a pair of baggy green pants. After Magda served us tea, Wainaina took out a thousand-shilling note, folded it, and gave it to the old woman to buy a cage for her chicken. She thanked us many times. "I will leave you to talk," she then said to no one in particular, and left holding her cup of tea.

I slipped a fifty-dollar bill into Magda's hands.

"American?" Magda said, smiling and looking at the bill.

I tried to apologize and explain that foreign exchange bureaus, legal or otherwise, were at every corner of this city. When she said "I know that," I realized she was talking about me.

"It's obvious you don't know me," she continued without waiting for the answer to her question. "And I am certain I have never worked with you."

Wainaina showed her his press card, explaining that we had been led here by her former workmate.

"Kamau is his name," I added.

"Oh, Kamau. You met him? Isn't he crazy? He is full of American this and that. So he was also fired? What happened?"

"Um, er, he didn't really want to talk about it," I said vaguely.

"Oh, Reverend, she's holy, you know," she said, and laughed. "You should attend the Festival of Rags. It's something."

"Are you going?"

"The festival is fun, but I don't think being poor is funny. Tell me, what do you want?" she said, looking at Wainaina.

"We are doing a story on Reverend Susan."

"You're going to nail her?" she said excitedly. "The fraud."

"We hope some good will come out of this. How long did you work for her?" he asked.

"About time someone did something. I started working for her about three years ago. I joined her church after my friend told me about it. The first day I went back home drunk with the word of the Lord and dreamed of angels. A band of angels once carried her home from America, you know."

"With angels and the Holy Spirit as her adviser," I said more to myself than to her, "she encountered no problems."

"Hmmm, not really. We are all human. I am not blind. I am not deaf. One sees things, hears things."

"What type of things?"

"It's difficult to put in words. Maybe I should start from the beginning. One Sunday after the service, I realized I had left my umbrella in the building. So I walked back to the hall. I found it closed. You see, I had gone some distance when I realized my loss. About twenty minutes, I would say. It's not their fault. But I did not want to lose my umbrella. So I walked around to the back. We had been told many times not to go in the back, because Susan spent her time in prayer and meditation."

"And conversation with angels," I said.

"I saw no angels, but sure, that's her time with the Holy Spirit."

"So, did you find the umbrella?" Wainaina asked.

"Let her tell it her way," I said to Wainaina; she looked at me as if to say I understood her better than this man.

"So I went around the back and knocked on the small black gate. Usually, she had a guard at the door, because sitting at the pews by the window, if you leaned forward, you could see the gate and a guard, next to the sign that said only authorized persons were allowed beyond the gate. But no one was answering, and as I tried to peep through the hole, I realized the gate was partially open. I stood there wondering if I should go inside or wait until someone came around. It was then that I heard some voices. I was so happy. I walked through the gate, toward the voices. As I turned the corner, I saw a few people, her most trusted and faithful, including the guard, standing in a circle of sorts. I hurried over, wondering if someone were sick. You know she claims to heal the sick. It was only when I got a bit closer that I realized they were trying to restrain a young woman. She was kicking and screaming, 'Please, Reverend, please . . . ' I thought she was possessed by the demons. The reverend can take out demons. Yes, that was it. The reverend seemed to be trying to calm her down, which is the first stage in exorcising demons. Make the possessed listen to you. Then command the demons. I heard something that made me think maybe it was not all about demons. 'Wangeci,' she said to the young woman, 'you signed the papers; there is nothing we can do now. You wanted him gone, and he has gone.' I had no idea what they were talking about. It was then that the reverend looked up and saw me. Everyone fell silent. They all stared back at me. You understand, don't you, that I didn't know what to do? I just stood there. 'What are you doing here? The service is over,' said the reverend to me, her eyes piercing mine. Oh, how I revered her. Shaky and nervous, I said, 'Oh, forgive me, Reverend, I left my umbrella in the hall and was wondering if someone found it.' 'You are not supposed to come back here, you know.' Though her eyes pierced me, her voice was ever so gentle. She was not angry. 'Can you go back and wait outside next to the black gate?' And off I went.

"Finally, she came and invited me into her office, apologizing for the commotion. 'Some demons are very obstinate,' she murmured. Then she asked if I had overheard anything. I lied, I don't know why, but I lied. Not that I thought anything sinister was going on. I was sure Wangeci was being a nuisance. I believed in the reverend.

"'Oh, to be a reverend is difficult sometimes,' she said to me, and proceeded to offer a cup of coffee. I happily accepted. She picked up her phone and asked the person on the other end to look for my umbrella in the lost and found. She was so kind.

"'Sorry about the mess in the office,' she said, pointing to a stack of files on the desk. 'It's hard to get a God-fearing reliable person to work here.' It was not messy. The files only needed to be put back on the shelves, but I did not question her definition of messy.

"'Where do you work?' she asked me. At the time I was jobless, having just undergone training with the GSU police force. But after the training was over, we were informed that the GSU was oversubscribed, so our services were not needed. All that training for nothing.

"Anyway, that's how I came to work for Reverend Susan. At the time I thought it was God's intervention."

"Why did you leave?" I asked.

"After working a year or two in that office, I started wondering, you know, about stuff."

"Like?" I nudged her.

"For one, I never saw her in prayer or meditation. But she was generous. I tried to turn my eyes, you know how you can look at something and tell yourself not to see, kind of— Don't write this," she said, turning to Wainaina, who promptly obeyed by putting his notebook and pen into his pocket.

"What was I saying? Yes, until I came across the baby files."

"Baby files? What do you mean?" I asked, my body suddenly taut.

"It was good that she opened the adoption center. At first it looked genuine. She took some children from the street and gave them shelter and food. She was doing a better job than our government. Then the white people started coming, and soon some of the children started to disappear. Rather, we stopped seeing them around.

"One day, Reverend Susan gave me a brown folder similar to the one in which I file all the church receipts. I opened it. She left with another folder. I opened the file; I always glanced inside the folders I filed. It was just a habit, curiosity, no harm. There was a list of women's names with X or Y marked next to them. Now, I would not have cared one way or another—Susan was all about business, really—except for the one woman whose name was in red. It occurred to me that the Wangeci I had seen when I first went to the reverend's office could have been the same one.

"Before I could read further, I heard Reverend Susan by the door. I quickly closed the file and pretended I was doing something else. She came straight toward me and took the file and said she had meant to take it but had taken the wrong one, the devil be cursed, and then asked in a casual way if I had opened the file. I said no, mine was to file, not to open files. After a few days she called me to her office and said that things had changed tremendously; she mumbled things about the economy and fired me. Not fired me, just like that; she gave my pay for the next three months. I tried to say I could work for free till the economy improved, but she said it was not fair to me, and thereafter she wouldn't even agree to see me."

"This Wangeci. Was there any other information about her? Age or where she lived?"

"All the women seemed to be in Kambera, but I don't know. There were no addresses, well, I guess there are no addresses in Kambera," she said, and laughed. "That's my story."

We thanked Magda greatly and left.

"I withdraw my comments of last night," Wainaina said as we walked back to the car. "Clearly, Susan does not profit by the light only. There is a lot more to Her Holiness than meets the eye."

"We have to meet with Wangeci," I told Wainaina.

"Yes, before we see the reverend. It makes sense."

"But how to find Wangeci?"

"Leave it to me," Wainaina said. "I'm a journalist. I have my sources."

14

I could do nothing about meeting Wangeci until Wainaina had found a contact. So the following morning, I called Zack. He did not answer, so I left a message telling him how we were enjoying South Africa.

Then Dr. Ciru called me from Cape Town. INTERPOL had been to her office. Police in in the States were looking for me, and they believed I was staying with her. Caught between the police interest and her loyalty to me, she opted for the space between truth and a lie: I had not yet arrived. Did she know where I was? they asked. No, she said, interpreting the question narrowly, and then added that she believed I was still on the way.

No sooner did I get off the phone than Sam called. Some detectives had interviewed Rosie about Zack's and my circle of friends. Rosie told them that I was a good person in a circle of bad people; she had even warned me against them, she said. She talked negatively about a Mark who bragged about his wealth and employed illegals. She could not understand why Joe had tried to kill me. Sam said that after they left, Ben was back with threats. He had found that I was not in Cape Town. It puzzled him that I had disappeared at about the same time as Zack and Melinda and Mark. Please call Ben or at least answer his calls, Sam pleaded with me.

I thought I had left New York behind. There were many issues I didn't understand—why, for instance, Mark would disappear and where he could be. Perhaps I should activate that hotline to Ben. I promised Sam I would and asked to talk with Rosie and Kobi. Rosie was bubbly about the interview and the fact that she had been able to pour her heart out. She was sure that Mark had gone into hiding to avoid answering questions about illegals. Sam was a great man. She and Sam loved Kobi. Sam's father blamed himself for not insisting that I carry a gun.

Kobi, the joy of my heart, told me he loved Mom and Dad in every other sentence. He did not sound anxious. He told me proudly that he had learned to pray and would be praying to Jesus to bring Mom and Dad home safely. The "praying to Jesus" Kobi must be the work of Rosie, I thought, or Sam or Sam's dad. Sam's dad could talk guns, gold, and God in the same breath.

Talking to Kobi lifted my spirits. His words reminded me that I had not yet visited my mother's place of rest. During the honeymoon, time had been taken up with seaside, sand, and glossy hotels. On the eve of our departure for Nairobi, we cut short the visit because Zack was needed in New York. My only memorial for my mother as the tears I had shed when I heard the news of her death. But they fell on the grounds of New York, not on her burial ground in Kenya.

I took a taxi to Kakuyu. Many thoughts whirled through my mind. It had startled me to hear Kobi talk of America as home, our home, so where was I? Why hadn't I come here before? Was it simply because of my abrupt departure, or was it that I could not possibly think of Kenya as home without my mother?

I thought a lot about my mother; her loving care; her stories; her proverbs meant to inculcate a moral or two in my obstinate head. She was particularly concerned about my endless questioning and hunger to know. When she warned that curiosity killed the cat, and I asked her how, she simply looked at me and said, "Continue acting on your curiosity, and you'll find out." "I don't want to die," I protested. "Then curb that curiosity." I promised. But when an Asian man walked into an elevator my mother and I were in, his hair looking so different than the kinky hair we had—his was like the mane of a horse—I suddenly felt rather than saw my arm dart out to the man's head. A patch of hair fell down, revealing the shiniest bald head I had ever seen. I now wanted to touch the baldness. My mother yanked my hand away. Fortunately, the elevator door opened, and the not too pleased gentleman walked out, ignoring my mother's apologies.

"You see, Mugure, curiosity seeks trouble, not knowledge. One does not have to act on the desire that killed a cat."

"Mother, whose cat? Ours?"

"Mugure, that's too many questions."

A lot had changed since I left my place of birth. Apartments had gone up on either side of the road. I was getting a little apprehensive as we neared the place where the house used to be, afraid of what it had become. Would the grave be there? Was there even a grave? My father had not bothered to let me know of the burial, and I had never reached out to find out.

I felt relief and gratitude when I found the marble grave at the back of the house, right in the middle of her herb garden. I sat down next to the grave. Looking at the herbs she so loved, I could feel her presence. Instead of the hollowness I had feared, I felt a sense of calm. I took a deep breath and surveyed the compound.

The garden intrigued me. The herbs were in bloom. I smiled at the memory of the many times my mother had tried to get me to do some garden work and the excuses I had perfected over the years. Wait. How was it that the herbs were still growing after all these years? And with no weeds. I jumped to my feet and looked around. To my utter surprise, I realized that the whole compound was immaculately clean and tidy.

Although all the doors were locked and the curtains drawn, the house did not look as if it had been abandoned. The paint had been retouched. I walked around the house, trying to get a peep inside for a sign or clue as to who lived here. The whole place had the feel of a diligently kept memorial to my mother. As far as I knew, my mother had no other children. Was it her ghost? I supposed I could ask the neighbors. Or I could go to the registration office, find its status, and initiate the process of reclaiming ownership. Surely my father knew. I would be seeing him as soon as I had sorted out the Kobi and Kasla business. That is, if I did not cut short my visit to quell the storm in Ohio.

Just then Wainaina called. He had found a contact, a woman named Betty.

• • •

As Jane drove us to Kambera to meet Betty, I thought maybe I should quit trying to find a vanishing local partner to yet another vanishing reality in New York, or a father I had never truly missed.

I was not cut out for this, as Ben had told me, even I knew that. All my life I had excelled at avoiding sticky situations. Unlike Jane, I had never been involved in a brawl in the street or school yard. It wasn't that I was afraid—unsure, yes, but not afraid. After all, my child's life was dependent on not being afraid to try. But I had to find the right balance between curiosity and caution, and maybe this venture called for more caution. But I did not call off the journey.

A beautiful hedge of bougainvillea with purple flowers and carefully trimmed edges marked the boundary between Living Green Estate and Kambera, but it did not prepare us for the dramatic contrast between the two. Living Green Estate was a pattern of spacious manicured lawns around sprawling houses. And Kambera? Built mostly from wood with patches of metal, grass, and mud, or any material that could seal a hole and hold together two or more pieces of wood or pipe, the Kambera houses were lined up next to each other, behind each other, on top of each other, with hardly any breathing space between.

We left our car at the Kambera parking garage and walked the rest of the way to Betty's. We sat on white plastic chairs covered with frayed cushions. The room was dark, hot, and humid. An unlit kerosene lamp sat in the corner of the mud floor. When a cool breeze blew in now and then, the curtain covering the small window flapped open, allowing more light into the room, momentarily supplementing the light that passed through the holes in the walls.

But for a musty smell, the room was spotlessly clean. A big cloth hanging in the middle separated the lounge-cum-kitchen from the bedroom. Incongruously, an uchu-matt tote bag hung on the wall next to a family photo. On a table tucked at the far side of the room were bottles of Tylenol.

Our host, a young woman wearing a brown maternity dress whom I guessed to be around twenty, sat across from us. Her pregnant belly seemed to overpower her, making her appear even weaker. She shyly accepted the bag of food we brought. She kept her eyes trained on the floor, mostly, and when she did look up, it was never at us but at the objects around the room.

"How far along are you?" I asked to break the awkward silence.

"A little over seven months." She saw me staring at the photograph on the wall. "That is my mother and my two siblings," she said. "Before the accident . . . Now I look at the picture and draw courage from it. I know I will make it."

We all murmured our condolences. The air, already tense, was now filled with sadness.

Wainaina gave her our names and then asked if she knew where and how we could find Wangeci; we were old friends who wanted to catch up with her. I could tell she was not convinced about the catching up, but she went along. "Wangeci doesn't live here anymore; she moved back to her mother's."

"Why?" I asked.

She hesitated and looked even more uncomfortable.

Suddenly, she raised her eyes and fixed them on me. It was my turn to squirm at finding myself the object of her gaze.

"We may be able to help her," I said, the first words that came to my mouth.

The woman remained emotionless, not removing her eyes from mine. She must have noticed my uneasiness. "I'm sorry, but for a second I thought you were her," she said.

"Me, Wangeci?"

"No, no, forget it. It was something, a look, the voice, this bad lighting, you know. These houses!"

The momentary tension, the suspension, subsided.

"So, you know Wangeci well?" I asked.

"We lived together in Kambera until she moved back home. I have not seen or talked to her since."

"Why did she move out?"

"You know, because of the baby."

"What happened?" I asked.

"Oh my goodness," she said, her turn to be shocked. "You mean you have no idea? When you said you were going to help her, I assumed you knew. You surely couldn't have heard of Wangeci's woes without knowing about the work."

"Betty, we have heard a little bit about her situation," I said sincerely. "But whatever made us come to you, it does not matter anymore. Not after hearing your story, your loss, the weight you carry, and yet thinking more about your friend than yourself. Please tell us everything. The work you do. How did you start it?"

Betty told us she worked at the Sheria Hotel, cleaning toilets, barely making enough to buy food for a week, as most of it went toward transportation. She was in so much debt that she even contemplated prostitution. Then a friend told her of a better job.

"What job?" Wainaina, Jane, and I asked in unison.

"Carrying babies for others is not easy. We go to Supa Duka fertility clinic in Mashingo. They put a man's seed into us." She sneezed and stopped to wipe her nose. I felt goose bumps less for her mention of in vitro fertilization than her matter-of-fact tone. She went on, "We visit the clinic twice. Health checkup and insemination. If we don't conceive, we go back. Otherwise we visit the clinic again, only at birth time. The pills you see over there, a man named Wakitabu brings them to us. Also the money."

"How many women are involved?"

"A lot, I would guess, but I don't know, except for the few who live here. We are like slaves, penned and fattened for our wombs. Not that they fatten us that much."

"This Wakitabu, when is he coming next?"

Betty was quiet for a moment. She was scared of him, she said. A few days ago, Wakitabu had arranged for her to go to the clinic because she'd complained of some pains; he'd thought she was about to deliver. She could not say what had overcome her, but she told the doctor she wanted to keep the baby. He told her she did not own the baby. Wakitabu came to her that evening to remind her that she was a paid overseer of another's property. Her threats of going to the police were met by threats.

"'You cannot play with other people's property,' he said, and showed me his police badge. Do you have children?" she asked, looking at us.

"For me, not yet," Wainaina said with a brief glance at Jane.

"Me, neither," Jane said, and looked at me as if she knew I was praying she wouldn't speak of her attitudes toward marriage and children.

"I have one. A boy," I said without elaborating.

"Then I don't need to tell you." Betty looked at me. "The bond between the mother and the baby she carries for nine months is very strong. In my case, pain and suffering have united us," she added with a touch of bitterness.

"The others, could they talk to us?" I asked as if this were part of our plan to help.

"Yes, but I would have to ask them first."

"Okay, we will stay in touch," Wainaina assured her, and again thanked her for receiving us and talking to us about a difficult experience. I stepped in and gave her some dollars.

"No, not American, I don't want to have to explain anything to Wakitabu."

Jane took out one or two thousand shillings and gave them to Betty. For baby clothes, she said. I had seen the terror in Betty's eyes every time she mentioned Wakitabu. There was the threat but something more as well. I asked, "Betty, tell me, why does Wakitabu terrify you so?"

She looked away for a few seconds and then back at me. "You don't understand. It's not the fear of loss of a child or death, even. It's being a slave for life. We cannot get out of the contract we signed freely. We have to keep on producing babies for as long as our bodies are able to—for life. We don't even feed our babies. They are taken from us as soon as we deliver them. We have three months of rest. Then another baby, sometimes multiple births, anywhere between two and eight. Our wombs have been hired for life."

It was chilling. We were so transported by her story that we almost forgot that we had come to find out how we could get in touch with Wangeci.

"Betty, can I ask you one more question? Was Wangeci one of the wombs for hire?"

"Her case was different," she said. "It's not as if she needed the job. But she can tell her own story herself. I never understood it fully."

"Will you help us get in touch with her?"

She stood up and studied me. "Can you really help her?" she almost whispered, with a bit more animation. "She was my friend. She is my friend. Will you really help her?"

Our eyes remained locked. Even the others noticed. Thoughts flashed through my mind. Why was I doing this? Merely to satisfy my curiosity? And then? Bye-bye, Kambera, Mugure has found the partner agency, reconciled the conflicting details on Kobi's adoption papers, and found her roots. It was me, me, me, all the way. Even my sudden passion for the roots must have been triggered by watching too much *Roots*. But at whose expense?

I thought of the recent calls from abroad and conceived of myself as a human wrecking machine. I had disturbed people's lives from Ohio to Manhattan to Cape Town. And now here! What right did I have to turn their lives upside down? Kasla may have had something to hide, and it was possible that my amateurish questions had stumbled upon something that the police had failed to see. The fact was, I could live without the details of Kobi's papers and without having to confront my father. I could put a stop to all the lot, Kasla, Mark, Joe's Mafia, my doubts, by ending the antics of a bored housewife and working harder to secure a material haven in a solid marriage. There was time for me to back out of this imbroglio with grace before I hurt more people. Besides, Betty had not really told us Wangeci's problem. However, my answer to the question was unequivocal.

"Yes!" I said firmly. "Yes, I will do my best."

15

People talk of epiphany as a religious experience, but what can I call what I had just gone through? Did I have to know the name of it? It was a question of faith. Betty had given me faith. Secular. Faith is a commitment to the as yet unknown, and whatever the name, I had given myself to something from which I couldn't back out and which was not solely about me.

Betty's saga of wombs for hire dominated dinner at Jane's house. The mood was introspective with none of the lightness of the previous ones. Our spoons and forks scraping the plates only emphasized the somberness. Finally, deep into the dinner, Jane broke the awkward silence.

"This is the worst case of assault on a woman's body that I have ever come across. Women forced to breed and their babies the property of some male assholes who didn't even sweat their penis in the process," she said, casting an eye at Wainaina. "Surrogacy is not a crime, but this is different. Cheap wombs. Enslaved wombs!"

"This society is sick," said Wainaina almost defensively.

"Kenya has remained the happy valley of the colonial yesterday—"

"Paradise," Jane interjected. "Wombs in paradise. A paradise of the crook and the crooked."

"My last investigative piece was on child pornography and pedophilia at the coast. Black madams selling underage girls to some aging fat white men for hard cash, sometimes under the cover of dance competitions in the big hotels and beach hostels. Unfortunately, the story was a one-week sensation. The government made some noise, threats of hell. The storm passes. There! Government goes back to sleep," Wainaina said.

"Government is male," Jane retorted. "Adam was the first government; Eve his first subject." She paused. "I'm sorry," she said, turning to Wainana. "You happen to be the only son of Adam present at the table." She leaned over and touched his cheek with her lips. "But you see my point? Eve seeks knowledge and passes the forbidden fruit to Adam, who readily accepts it. They are expelled from paradise. Eve is sentenced to bear children with pain, while Adam paces about the yard, waiting to claim ownership. Mugure, my views on marriage and children were formed a long time ago, as you know. Call it my rebellion against the sentence on women. That's really why I became a lawyer, not because of Portia in *The Merchant of Venice*. Portia was inserting herself in a battle of property between thieving males. I wanted to defend women against the original sentence. Not that it's easy, no, it's not. I tell you, every time I bang my head against a government's intrusion in women's rights, I end up bleeding. We three were witnesses to a crime, at least the compelling testimony of a crime. I am a defense attorney. We don't prosecute. That's the work of law enforcement. Of course, if clients come to us, we can initiate civil suits."

"I thought that as FIDA, you were proactive when it came to women's empowerment—or in this case, women's disempowerment," I said.

"We are, but we still have to work within a male system. And in that system, women have nowhere to hide, not in their homes, not in the government, not in churches, mosques, or temples. I've always thought of Atlas as a woman carrying the weight of the globe. That's why one has to admire Reverend Susan, making it in a man-eat-man system—sorry, I should say man-eat-woman society. But even she ends up maintaining the male system."

I had never seen Jane in this mood. She had always been a fighter, a doer, not Miss Hamlet. It was clear that Betty had touched a raw nerve in Jane.

"Ah, my friend Mugure. As a defense lawyer, I am driven by the ideals of helping to maintain a fair system of rules, whether it results in a win or a loss in a particular case. But this assumes a delicate balance of policing, investigation, prosecution, defense, judgment, and enforcement. What if it turns out that Wakitabu is in charge of all the elements? My friends, I cannot sit here and pretend that the case of *Republic* versus *Alternative Clinics* did not leave bruises, and they have not yet healed."

"What happened?" I ask.

"As you know, abortion in this country is illegal. But for one reason or another, women are aborting. Along come the Mary Magdalene Sisters. They form an NGO, Alternative Clinics, for a humane solution to the illegal abortions. They encourage women and young girls to carry the baby to full term and then give up the babies for adoption.

Basically, they provided an expectant mother with all the essentials she needed to ease the pregnancy. They provided free education for some of the girls. According to Alternative Clinics, only about half the women chose to give up the babies. These were placed in government or government-supervised adoption centers."

"Sounds like a noble project," I said.

"The brain behind the whole thing is Sister Paulina. From all accounts, it seemed to work well. She wanted to expand to HIV centers. "

"A kind of local initiative," Wanaina said.

"Yes, that was the beauty of it. Sister Paulina had the same kind of background as Susan. In fact, she comes from the village next door; the women are almost mirror images. Bright. Attractive. Forceful personalities and, in their own way, dedicated to serving others. But Paulina chose a different path: the Roman Catholic way. That way enables what she loves most: education. She admires the selflessness of nuns, and she decides to become one, in short, working within an established system to give back a little of that which was given to her. Within the Catholic Church, she sees room for individual initiative, in the tradition of all those orders from the Jesuits of old to the orders of Irish missionaries. For Sister Paulina, from what I could gather, working within a system ensured removing herself from any temptations of personal gain. The programs start receiving recognition. Visitors from Brazil to India flock, even some who used to work with Saint Teresa in the streets of Calcutta. The model is seen as one that could be copied elsewhere."

"We carried stories about some of these visitors," Wainaina confirmed. "We did a profile of Sister Paulina with the sensational heading: 'The Black Teresa: On Path to Sainthood.'"

"That article could have been the beginning of the end of the Alternative Clinics," Jane said, again turning to Wainaina, who frowned, but she ignored it and continued. "I mean, the article and its prominence may have set the problems in motion. At first they were rumors—that the Alternative Clinics were not what they seemed. Then Susan gave the rumors a leg and a voice—the clinics were encouraging young girls to have early sex. The chorus was taken up by all the other churches, Protestant, of course."

"Yes," added Wainaina. "I remember interviewing the head of the PCEA Nairobi chapter. He almost foamed at the mouth as he denounced the clinics, asserting that this hypocrisy has been the real face of Roman Catholicism since the times of Pope Leo X, who declared war on Luther."

The government had taken the clinics to court on charges of unspecified illegal activities. LAW took up the defense and sent their top lawyer. Jane demanded that the republic stop trying her clients in the press; she also sought specifics of the charges and a list of witnesses.

"What happened in court?" I asked.

"Four things: Father Brian, a document, the Vatican, and Detective Mbaya," Jane said with an enigmatic smile that barely hid her bitterness.

"Mbaya, as in Swahili for bad?" I asked. Jane nodded.

Detective Mbaya had told the court that he intended to prove crimes of commission and prospective commission. Leading the list of witnesses was Father Brian, and for proof, a document so sensitive and explosive in its claims that its contents could not be revealed in court. Yet the document contained the only evidence of prospective crime. Jane had a fierce exchange with Detective Mbaya, headlined in the press as "Kagendo Faces Mbaya," with their pictures glaring at each other on the front page. The case never went ahead; the Vatican intervened. The clinics were closed. Sister Paulina was called to the Vatican. And then relieved of her order.

Jane stopped to drink some water, though I suspected it was to calm her emotions. "The papers ran with the story: 'The Fall of a Saint,'" she said.

"One thing we could not understand," Wainaina said. "Mbaya had a fairly good reputation in a force that had lost credibility since the debacle of the Armenian brothers accused of smuggling guns into the country. But he seems to have lived true to his bad name."

"I used to have so much respect for him. Not so much after that," Jane said. "Out of the fiasco emerged clear losers and winners. I lost. My star—sorry, Wainaina—was no longer shining. Nor was Sister Paulina's. She was the other loser. I was too ashamed to face her afterward. It was as if I had let her down."

"I tried to get an interview for the *Daily Star,*" Wainaina said. "Apparently, she had been sworn to silence by the Vatican in exchange for continuing her service within the Catholic fold. She now teaches in Msongari."

"Our old school," Jane and I said in unison.

"We could talk to her. Years have passed. She may be willing to share some information," I suggested.

We agreed. Jane offered to make the arrangements and then continued, "The clear winners were Reverend Susan and Father Brian. Reverend Susan registered her adoption agency: the Real Alternative Clinics. Father Brian became a sensational picture of morality, although nobody knew what it is he had wanted to say in court. Some rumors claimed that he was the author of the secret document that doomed the clinics and brought about the fall of a saint. Brian became an overnight celebrity when he registered his all-purpose charity to lift Africa. Some called him a great nationalist, a white Pan-Africanist even, a holy visionary. Madness! How could a name like All Lost African Sun Kingdoms Arise turn a wayward priest into a Pan-Africanist visionary overnight?"

"Extraordinary," I said. "A whole sentence for the title of a mere charity?"

"It's registered under the initials," Wainaina said. "ALASKA. Alaska Enterprises!" He looked at me as if he had realized the implication.

"Oh my God," I said, excusing myself to the bathroom, where I sat motionless, though my mind was a whirlwind. How did Alaska Enterprises end up in my husband's file in Riverdale? Whatever, the saga of the Alternative Clinics and Betty's story of enslaved wombs were intertwined with my life. I played with the initials. Alaska. Kalaska. Kasla. The Palmer defense of Kasla. Rhino Man. The priest. The gunman. The priest, the lawyer, the gunman, and the Rhino Man. Mark. Joe. The Mafia. A web of intrigue and personalities. How did they connect?

I took out my cell phone to call Ben. I had forgotten to keep my phone on. He had called again. Ben . . . but why was he following me? Was he part of the web? I decided not to call him just yet. I had to find out more, arm myself with details, knowledge. I had to take a good look at this Wakitabu and the Supa Duka, the fertility clinic in Mashingo, and anything else connected with Alaska. Then meet with Paulina, Wangeci, and Susan. In that or any other order.

"I am going to Kambera," I told Jane and Wainaina after I returned to the table.

They looked at each other, then at me.

"For a few days," I added.

16

The next call from Ohio sounded anxious. Ben had called Sam again to tell him they had questioned Joe and found that his story didn't make sense. Nor did the fact that I'd ended up in Ohio and then disappeared, leaving Kobi behind. Ben wanted to know the relationship between Joe and Sam and sounded skeptical when Sam denied knowing Joe. What irritated Sam was Ben's implication of a white conspiracy against a black female.

"Oh, and Dad advises you to get a gun. He does not like this Ben fellow insinuating that I could be involved in the disappearance of an African queen," he said with a nervous chuckle.

I had to stop this. This time I called Ben.

"Mugure, thanks for calling. Where are you? I have been looking for you everywhere."

"And harassing my friends? Threats, even?"

"You must admit that the series of events has been strange. I am your friend, sister. I meet with you at Kennedy. We talk about Zack and suited gunmen. I give you my hotline for any emergency. The same afternoon, you leave your home in Riverdale in such a hurry that you don't even stop at traffic lights. Thereafter, Joe chases you all the way to Manhattan. He calls us. I question him, and he tells me some fiction that you are crazy. But you did not look crazy to me when we met at the airport. He says we should lock you up in a ward to have your head examined. Then you vanish. You leave behind a child you love. Cape Town? You are not there. My calls to you? No response. Melinda disappears at about the same time. The police ask Mark to report at the police station to answer a few questions about smuggling and employing illegal immigrants. He disappears. You told me that he recommended Kasla to you. Kasla was once represented by Palmer. I drive past the curio shop. The owner is gone."

"The Rhino Man?" I asked, unable to disguise my fear.

"Is that what you call him? Mugure, we have to meet. There are things I want to tell you."

"Ben, I am far away. Can't you can tell me over the phone?" I asked.

"A meeting is best."

The more he emphasized a meeting, the more suspicious he made me, but curiosity overrode that. What if he was telling the truth? I did not want him to bother Sam again. "I am in Kenya," I said.

"What! You are in Kenya?" he sounded agitated.

"I was going to South Africa. I changed my mind at the airport."

"Remember my friend Johnston, the detective I once told you about? I will text you his number. He is a good man. Please call him in case of anything . . . Mugure, I'm sorry, but I must ask you this: Has Zack been in touch with you lately?"

"Why? Has anything happened to him? Please tell me."

"I don't know. We lost him in Tallinn. We think he may have crossed over to Latvia."

"What about the suited gunman?"

"We haven't seen him, either. Does Zack know you are in Kenya?"

Why does he want to know? I asked myself. "No!" I said.

"Keep it that way."

"Look, Ben, tell me the truth. Is Zack safe?"

"Put it this way: I'm not aware of any harm to him."

"Thank you for your concern, but I really have to go now," I said, trying to terminate the conversation without unduly annoying him. I could not trust him fully. His good came mixed with evil. Perhaps he wanted his friend—if Detective Johnston existed—to keep an eye on me.

"Wait. How about Melinda?" he asked.

"She is performing at the annual Festival of Rags. Look, I have to attend to something now," I said hastily, and hung up.

I called Zack. No response. At least Ben had not said anything about the suited gunman hurting him. I will keep on trying, I said to myself, both upset and relieved that I did not reach Zack.

But the fact that I did not know where he was, along with the conversation with Ben, left me with more questions than answers, including his role in the mess. Why did Mark's friend Joe want me locked up in a ward? And why had Mark disappeared? Where had the Rhino Man gone? I felt like I was lost in a maze where everything was visible, even familiar, but each path I took ended in a cul-de-sac, and I had to retrace my footsteps to the beginning.

I must get to the bottom of it. I felt comfortable with my decision to spend a few days and nights in Kambera.

Betty waited for me at the bus stop. Her belly seemed to have grown bigger within the last twenty-four hours, but she looked less overwhelmed by it, maybe because of the bright flowery maxidress she wore. She had a pretty face, despite the hardships that she bore on her thinning shoulders. Her braided hair was held back in a ponytail that made her head look a little pointed, but the style suited her well. She smiled broadly when she saw me, then covered her mouth with her hand when I removed my head scarf.

"Oh my, you cut your hair off? You look so different, but I like it." She had said exactly what I needed to hear. That was why I had cut it short. To get rid of the lady from the Bronx.

Last night's revelation had made me feel a more personal relationship with Kambera. As we walked back to Betty's place, I noticed what I hadn't the first time—the many women who sat outside creating hairdos that were really works of art. At my request, Betty had arranged for me to meet a few other women in the scheme. And of course, Wakitabu.

Betty first took me to see Grace Atieno, who lived about a fifteen-minute walk from Betty. She was a vibrant and extremely beautiful woman. She and her parents had been chased from their home in Naivasha. Her parents lived in the IDP camps. But she had to help them and her younger siblings. Unlike Betty, Grace did not care if people knew how she earned her living. She took the view that she was rendering a positive service to childless couples. "I just take care of their child for nine months and then leave the rest to them. It's like babysitting, except easier, because the baby is in my belly. Some women are paid for wet nursing; I am paid for carrying them. I bring a little happiness to childless couples."

In the early evening, Betty walked me to Philomena Wanjikū's. Philomena's father had been killed in post-election violence in Molo. Her mother lived in IDP camps. She had left to the city in order to provide for her three siblings and see them through school. Her story and Grace Atieno's were almost interchangeable.

She was preparing dinner when we arrived. The kitchen was also the living room, and we sat there. The small house was sparsely furnished with the bare necessities: a table and three wicker chairs. On her wall, she had old ragged pictures of African American musicians pulled from newspapers and magazines. The King of Pop, Michael Jackson, took center stage, while a refreshingly young Whitney Houston graced the left wall, a picture so innocent that it exemplified the beauty of her voice before drugs removed her from music grace.

Philomena had been working several jobs and could hardly meet expenses when she heard about the wombs for hire and jumped at the opportunity. "Giving away that first child, my own blood, was not easy, but I needed the money. I really wouldn't encourage you to go through with it. You see, the baby I gave away, I think about her all the time. I know she is in America, or at least that's what they told me, so maybe her life is better there. But there are the small things. Does she resemble me in any way? This is the second baby, but I can't go through with the arrangement. I thought I could, but I can't. I want to keep the baby. I must."

She was quiet for a few minutes and then looked up. I thought she was wondering whether to trust me.

"I plan to run away into the rural areas. They are very powerful people. But I will find a way. Even a hare is able to outsmart the bigger animals."

I was going to add that these were animals of prey, then stopped: If art gave her hope and the courage she needed to go through with it, who was I to intrude with facts of a situation I hardly understood? Story. Song. Dance. Whistling, all plentiful in Kambera streets and houses. The images pasted on the walls afforded her moments of escape into dreams.

Later in the evening, Philomena showed me a tiny room with two single beds. "Your bed, my bed," she said, and laughed. There was something endearing about laughter amid the squalor. Laughter embodied resistance against agents of gloom.

Some noise woke me up in the middle of the night, and I saw that Philomena's bed was empty. I wondered where she might have gone and then remembered that the communal toilets were outside. I relaxed and settled back into the rather uncomfortable bed. The mattress was so thin, I could feel the springs under my back.

Then: "I told you, you can meet her in the morning," I heard Philomena complaining.

I panicked, but before I could get out of bed properly, I saw a burly figure standing at the door to the bedroom.

"Who are you?" I asked, trying hard to control my shaky voice.

"Who *are you*?" the man retorted and started toward me.

He looked scary. Just then Philomena, in her blue cotton nightdress, stepped forward, a flashlight in her hand,

and stood between us. But before she had finished saying, "Amina, this is Wakitabu," the man had brushed her aside and was in my face. He grabbed me by the collar and pulled me close. His breath was a nasty mix of fish and cigarettes. I could see a scar above his eye; his receding hair was beginning to turn gray. I was now half sitting and half floating in the air. I could barely breathe, let alone talk.

"What do you want with Betty and Philomena?" he demanded.

"I . . . I have no job . . . I . . . want to join," I attempted to say.

He had probably been following me around and knew I was Mugure. "Join what? Who told you?"

"The women . . . Betty . . . she's my cousin. She told you," I insisted.

He suddenly let go of my collar, and I fell on the bed. He stood by the bed, still looking as if he would punch me. "You go to the clinic tomorrow. If you so much as breathe a word to someone else, I will not spare you next time." He pulled some rumpled papers from his back pocket, straightened them out on his lap as if ironing them, and then shoved them toward me. "Print your name here and then sign!"

I could barely see what it was I was signing. Philomena shone the flashlight on the paper, and I was able to make out "now property of Alaska Enterprises."

"I didn't say read, I said sign," he barked at me.

I did and handed him the paper, which he folded and stuffed into his back pocket. When he got to the door, he shouted, "By the way, you will get a third of what's due to you, another third when you conceive, and the rest when the baby is born. If you want more money, they can impregnate you with eight," he said, and laughed.

And with that, the dreaded Wakitabu was gone. Phi-lomena closed the door after him and apologized for his behavior. She didn't have to; I understood perfectly that they needed to scare me half to death to make me feel that my every move was being watched, in the process making me sign my life away. Even Ben was trying similar tactics.

I started to cry. I felt hemmed in from all sides in Amer-ica and Kenya by forces I could not comprehend. I needed to go back to my mother's grave to find peace. Then I re-membered her admonition that one must walk with the head held high and back straight, because slouching bent one's body and spirit. I was my mother's daughter. That made me feel better. I was not sure if I wanted to go to the Supa Duka, but I could not quit. It was a crucial part of the dots I was trying to connect.

17

The town where the Supa Duka was located was nick-named Donkey City. From the moment I got off the bus, I understood why. Donkeys were everywhere. I had to fight my way through lines of carts piled high with all sorts of goods, from used tires and sacks bulging with po-tatoes to white aluminum tanks. The starved gray beasts of burden shat and brayed as if in competition, and I walked gingerly to avoid stepping on a mound. I almost laughed when I recalled Kamau telling us about the demons that Susan had cast out from the bodies of the possessed. Had they relocated here?

The town could as easily have gone under the name Condom City. From the shopfronts on either side of the main street hung condom posters. Not just the shops on the main street but the whole town: Every wall was pasted with bills advertising Proctor condoms. Looking at the long-haul trucks parked along the roads, with young half-naked girls circling around them, I could guess why the condom was the dominant decor in this town built during the colonial era and which, by all indications, seemed to have resisted growth. The condom was the only sign of modernity, but then it also brought to mind the modernity of HIV.

I was actually happy to step into the Supa Duka, if only to escape the dust and wind. My eyes were burning and felt as if someone were pushing little pebbles into them. But once I was inside the premises, the prospect of what I was about to do hit me. What was the difference between me and the half-naked girls circling the trucks? If they could escape the virus by using the condom, their ordeal was brief if brutish, and I supposed one could always say, "No, not tonight." But these others had to carry the pain of humiliation through nine months and then a lifetime of scars of the body and spirit. I was not here to play philosopher but to probe, I reminded myself. How far was I willing to go? The question loomed large. I wasn't sure. I hadn't planned this through. I had to proceed cautiously—ensuring, for instance, suppression of any trace of an American accent—but then I remembered that every youth in Kenya, even those who had never left the country, tried versions of Americanism. As for insemination, I was well aware that that they did not do the operation on the first meeting. But suppose they had changed their routine? I would have to insist that I had understood it differently or fight my way out, I told myself, recalling my training in martial arts.

The doors were open, so I stepped right in to face a balding man who sat on the counter reading a magazine. It looked like a normal general shop with all manner of items, mostly over-the-counter drugs, on half-empty shelves. I got confused and felt foolish, especially when the man looked at me from head to toe without moving.

"Daktari. Are you the doctor?" I asked timidly.

He rolled his eyes and pointed toward a blue metal door past the counter and went back to his magazine, which, I noted as I passed, was upside down. I took a deep breath and turned the doorknob. The door swung open, revealing a blue room. It held the smell I always associated with hospitals and medicine. There was nobody behind the reception desk. I heard some voices. When I stepped closer to listen, my heart was pounding. The voices and movement in the other room got louder, and before I could make out what was going on, a woman wearing a dark green uniform walked in.

"What are you doing here?" she asked.

"Wakitabu sent me here. My name is Amina."

"Your ID, please," she said as she stepped behind the reception desk.

"ID? I don't have one. I mean, er, I didn't bring one. Wakitabu didn't tell me to carry one."

"You need a man to tell you to carry your ID? You women . . . Now, how in the world am I going to know if you are the Amina you say you are?"

"Why don't you call Wakitabu?"

"Go home and come back tomorrow. With your ID," she said without looking up.

I started to walk out, but at the door, I heard a man's voice call out, "Simama!" I turned around to face a man with a huge Afro, looking for all the world as if he had stepped out of the sixties. His long white coat fell over brown corduroy bell-bottoms and a white turtleneck. A stethoscope hung from his neck. He introduced himself as Daktari, the Swahili name for doctor. "Bring the ID next time," he said to me.

He asked me to sit down on a wooden bench in the reception area while he remained standing in front of me. "So, Amina, why do you want to do this?"

"I need the money. I don't want to have to join the ranks of those hovering around the truck drivers."

"Well, you will certainly make more here than those little whores. They give women a bad name." He said this with arrogance.

"How much will I get?" I was trying to sound more confident than I felt.

"Didn't Wakitabu tell you?"

"No, he said I should discuss it with Alaska," I lied, to see if I could get more information.

"He told you that? Alaska?"

"The papers that I signed said Alaska," I answered vaguely.

"Wakitabu will bring your money to you. I don't discuss money," he said, and I made a mental note that he had not elaborated on Alaska. "But I can tell you this, if they are twins, you get double. So pray for twins," he said without any emotion.

"And if I get six? Wakitabu suggested eight."

"The more you carry, the more you get," he said, "but let's take it step by step. Are you ready?" He got up and motioned for me to follow him, which I did through the back door.

"Are there side effects or complications that I need to be aware of?" I asked. "I hear that the uterus can collapse . . . pro—"

"Prolapsed uterus," he said, proud to show his knowledge. "Rare, but it can happen. Everything has risks."

"I want to do this until I meet my needs. One woman

told me that once I start, I can't get out of it. Am I in it for life?"

"You sure do ask a lot of questions. But we are professionals, my dear; don't you worry your head about it." He looked at me quizzically. "It's all in your contract," he added as an afterthought.

"Wakitabu took it with him."

"It's safe. But it does not deal with illnesses."

I felt prickly heat under my arms. As I reached up to ward off the itch, I realized my hands were shaky. I had to keep my composure. I looked at everything, trying to make mental notes without appearing unduly curious. Finally, he led me through yet another door into a huge room filled with all sorts of medical equipment. In the middle of the room was a bed with overhead lighting. A state-of-the-art theater in Donkey City? Betty and Philomena had not been hallucinating.

A woman in a white coat who I guessed was the assistant stood by a bed at the far end of the room. The table seemed reserved for birthing. The man gave me blue overalls to put on. He pointed at a curtain and told me to change in there.

My heart raced. What if they knew I was Mugure and they were toying with me? What if I went on the examining bed and they injected me with something that induced permanent sleep? My son. Kobi. Would I ever see Kobi again?

"Everything, your jeans, remove everything," the woman was saying.

"You may also want to use the bathroom before heading out this way," shouted the doctor, pointing at a small door on my right.

The minute he said so, I felt the need to go badly. I half ran into the bathroom, a small clean space that smelled of disinfectant. My mind was racing. How was I going to get out of this now? I had made out okay so far, but I needed an exit strategy. Damn, I should have thought of this before. No time to panic . . . think! I felt so much freer after peeing. I washed my hands and walked back to face the consequences, wringing my hands to dry them.

"Relax, today is just the examination," Daktari assured me as he gestured to the bed with his gloved hands. "When you come back next month, we will plant the seeds."

He and his assistant were now in scrubs and face masks. The operating room was lit more brightly, and the temperature seemed cooler.

As I climbed on the bed, I tried to read the doctor's eyes to catch signs of anything sinister. My body was screaming at me to run, but I willed myself to put my feet in the stirrups and lie down, readying myself for the ordeal.

The doctor pulled out a handheld device that resembled a microphone, and poured some lubricant on it. I had been to enough clinics to know that he was going to do a transvaginal ultrasound. As I watched the doctor get ready to insert the gadget in my privates, I tried to think other thoughts, which had worked for me in other clinics, but I could not escape the reality: This doctor probing my uterus was a criminal.

When I heard the doctor say, "You can get dressed," I rushed to put on my clothes. The nurse tried to explain something about the next visit, but I could hardly wait to get out. I felt as if I would suffocate. I longed to breathe the air that I had so detested two hours earlier.

I welcomed the dust, the donkey carts, the shit, the

braying. I could not understand why there was so much secrecy surrounding the Supa Duka, unless it was a cover for something that embraced more than the mass production of children for adoption. Then I heard a commotion from the market square. I was so glad to see so many people that I hastened toward them as if they had come out in big numbers for me. "What is going on here?" I asked a woman.

"Husband and wife are fighting over their kids," she said.

I stood on tiptoe and saw a man with a stick in his right hand, fuming with anger. Standing in front of him was a white man shielding a woman. The woman would hurl a few choice insults at her fuming husband and then duck behind the gray-haired white protector, who spoke fluent Kiswahili, trying to calm the irate husband, in which he had succeeded, because husband and wife were now talking civilly.

"Who is that?" I asked a woman, referring to the white man.

"That is Father Brian," she said as if this were an everyday scene in the community. "Very nice man. When he is not teaching cricket, he runs a food program for children. When we are in trouble with our men, we run to him," she said, and laughed.

I felt like I was staring at a well-known character who had emerged from a novel to walk among the living. I edged closer to take a good look at the man who had brought down the Alternative Clinics and even forced the hand of the Vatican, the visionary founder of Alaska Enterprises whose tentacles had reached my house in the Bronx. What would happen if I were to walk over and demand that he explain himself? How a piece of paper with "Alaska Enter-prises" on it came to be in my husband's office and his car? But I had my cover to protect.

I started walking toward the bus stop, lost in thought. Then I felt a presence walking beside me and turned my head. It was Father Brian.

"What a surprise, Father," I said, stopping to face him. "It's nice of you to bring domestic peace."

"It's my calling," he said. "But I sometimes bring war. Are you American?" He was so incredibly soft-spoken, so soothing, that I almost forgot the gravity of the question, the answer, and the situation.

"No," I said, smiling.

"He sent you to snoop, right?" he asked.

"Who? What are you talking about?" I asked.

He dug into his pocket and removed a piece of paper that he handed to me. I unfolded it and suddenly felt vulnerable. I was staring at a photo of Zack and me outside Shamrock on our last visit. The day of the suited gunman. My heart skipped a beat. I stepped back.

"You don't want die for another," he intoned. "Christ did that for us all. Tell him he can hide behind your skirts, but he can't hide from me."

I was looking down and around, unsure what to do or say. When I looked back in the priest's direction, he had vanished back among his adoring crowd. I hastily walked to the bus stop and got inside the Nairobi-bound *matatu*.

When I got to Jane's house, it was early evening. I had to speak to Jane or Wainaina. The coincidence of my having told Ben that I was in Kenya and then finding out Father Brian knew me was too much to take. I recalled my meeting with Ben at Kennedy. He knew about the altercation with the suited gunman outside Shamrock. Now Father Brian had a picture of the same event.

The door to Jane's bedroom was wide open. I walked in to find Wainaina's arms wrapped around Jane. Wow. Jane and Wainaina?

"Sorry, didn't mean to intrude," I said, and before they recovered their composure, I retreated into the kitchen and started making coffee. I was not sure how I felt. I recalled the close encounters between Wainaina and me, but I got ahold of myself. Jane was my best friend, after all. Right now there were other urgent matters.

Jane and Wainaina joined me in the kitchen. I told them about the clinic and about Brian and his chilling message.

"This is getting creepy," Wainaina said.

"And dangerous," Jane added. "The good news is that Betty has texted Wangeci's number."

The next morning I called Ben, just to know where he was. I then called Zack. Still no answer.

I called Wangeci and set up a meeting at her place the same day.

18

Jane dropped off Wainaina and me at Kenyatta Avenue, where we hired a taxi. Maina, the driver, was a chubby fellow who claimed that Nairobi would become a huge parking lot if nothing were done to ease the traffic jam. Talking all the while, he used back streets to get us onto Limuru Road in good time.

In Tigoni, we were welcomed by spacious houses with well-manicured gardens surrounded by carefully trimmed hedges and driveways lined with palm trees. We passed by Tigoni Dam and pulled up at gate 5 on Kilesho Drive. The black iron gate with indecipherable artwork was attached to a high brick wall that ran across the curbside. Maina rang the bell, and after a while, we heard a clanking noise. The electric gate begun to slide open, disappearing into the wall to reveal a massive gray house surrounded by a lush green lawn.

We left Maina in the car outside. Wainaina and I walked toward the door through a veranda filled with potted plants. A girl, about eight years old, welcomed us into the house and led us to the living room. Something about her looked familiar, but I was not able to put my finger on it. The decor was appalling: Every manner of couch in gray and blue filled the otherwise spacious room. Two women sat near the middle of the room, and as soon as they saw us, they started to rise. The older of the two was heavyset. She must have weighed about three hundred pounds, and she panted with the attempt to rise.

"You don't have to get up," I said, walking toward them.

"My child, I have to greet my visitors," she said. Using her hands on the couch armrests to balance herself, she was on her feet finally.

A younger woman who turned out to be Wangeci walked toward us as well. "Hey, come and greet our visitors," she called to the little girl, who was standing behind Wainaina. "This is Mwihaki, my other daughter's little girl."

Mwihaki said "how are you" from a distance. "You look like Auntie Wangeci," she added, and disappeared. Wangeci laughed and introduced herself.

"I am Wangeci's mother," the older woman said. "I don't see the resemblance Mwihaki is talking about. But your skin is dark and beautiful."

"Thank you. I am Mugure, and this is the journalist Wainaina." We shook their hands.

"Oh, Wainaina," she said, and burst into a hearty laugh. "I know you, though we have never met. You are a brave man. Thanks for the good work you do."

Wangeci, lean, dark, and strikingly beautiful, came across as shy. Her smiling eyes belied what she may have gone through. She went back to where she had been sitting. Her legs on the couch, she reached for a blue cushion and held it across her chest. The mother fussed around us and gave us tea and juice before she sat down again.

I chose the couch nearest to Wangeci and her mother. "Thank you for agreeing to meet us on such short notice," I started. Wangeci didn't answer but kept her gaze on me. "We understand you are part of the wombs for hire?"

"Sort of. I never really was," she corrected me.

"Sorry. What . . . um . . . what had you joined? How did you, um, I mean, how did you get involved? Did someone recruit you?"

"Betty had told me about it."

"She always was out with the wrong crowd," her mother quipped.

"Mooooom," Wangeci chided her.

"She thought it was an easy way of raising money," her mother continued.

"I had run away from home," Wangeci said, looking at her mother.

"Why?" I asked.

"My mother here never let me do anything on my own. I felt like a prisoner," she said.

"It's hard to bring up a child with an absent father!"

"I resented having a father who never showed up," Wangeci said.

Sounded familiar. I thought of asking about the absent father, then dismissed it.

"When I came home and found her gone, I cried for a whole week," Mama said. "Then I thought it would be a good lesson for her to learn, and oh my God, did she learn it the hard way."

"Anyway," Wangeci continued after giving her mother a dirty look, "Betty took me along to meet this guy Wakitabu, a kind of go-between, whom I instantly disliked. I dismissed the very thought of carrying a baby, but I needed the money. I wanted to show my mother I was capable of taking care of myself. I didn't give an answer right then. And then I met him, and everything changed."

"Who?"

"Excuse me, but the thought of him, his name, makes me sick," she said, visibly shaken.

I let her compose herself.

"I met him a few days after Wakitabu. He laughed off the idea of my carrying babies. He wanted me in his life. He projected a caring personality. He had the money; there was no need for me to work. We fell in love, I moved into his apartment in Green Estate, and before long, he was talking of my joining him in America."

Wainaina and I exchanged glances. It was our first direct American connection, unlike Kamau's generic American.

"Was he American?" I asked, all alert.

"Yes, of course," she said. "I had not met a person who loved life so much, which was really what I needed at that age. And the American promise. I became pregnant. We didn't want to keep the baby, but we differed on what to do about it. I wanted to abort, but he convinced me it was better to give the baby away than to abort it. Almost like the way those clinics used to do. He told me the baby would go to a caring wealthy couple, part of a millionaire club for babies," she said, and laughed almost in a sneer.

When she got to the sixth month, she changed her mind. She wanted to keep the baby. He became upset, telling her that the baby had already been promised to a high-powered politician in Washington. He told her he had big plans for them, and the unplanned baby would interfere with the big picture of expanding his empire to the rest of Africa and Asia. That was why he was always on the move, sometimes gone for days. A multi-businessman, he had good connections to top government officials, judging by the license plates of the cars that would sometimes drop him by the Green Estate apartment.

"I did not understand why he was so keen on giving up our baby, seeing that we were still a couple," Wangeci said, "and he was rich."

She fretted, asked questions, particularly about the wombs for hire and if he had something to do with it. He denied any links to it. How, then, did he know about the millionaire club for babies? Or that the baby had been promised to a Washington politician? He looked her in the eye and told her, for their own flesh and blood, he had gone to the most trustworthy adoption agency: the Real Alternative Clinics, now the Miwani.

"You mean the one owned by Reverend Susan?" Wainaina asked.

"Yes, Her Holiness."

"I have never trusted that woman and her miracles and angels," Mama Wangeci said. "I know her village . . ."

"I continued to assert my rights to the baby. I wanted us to marry. I told him I would go to the newspapers. I was just saying, but I was surprised by how the threat changed his approach. He relented and said I could keep the baby. The wedding would follow the baby's birth. I was so happy."

A week before her due date, Wangeci felt ill, a mixture of nausea and extreme thirst that could not be quenched by water. She insisted they go to hospital, but the man brought her some juice and said it would make her feel better. A few sips and her condition worsened. She could not say what had happened; all she remembered was waking up with a sharp pain across her belly in a clinic with the man and the doctor by her side.

They told her that she had been in a coma, and fearing for her life and the baby's, they had been forced to operate. Her baby was stillborn, and they had buried it. She did not believe them and kept on screaming, demanding to see her baby or the grave. The doctor forcefully injected her with a drug to calm her. When she came around, she was in the rented apartment alone. The man—or the American, as she now called him—had packed all his things and vanished. She had no one to call.

Dazed, she walked across the bougainvillea hedge that divided the Green Estate and Kambera. Betty was the only friend she had, and the name of the one person the American had mentioned. She went to Reverend Susan. The reverend insisted that Wangeci had signed papers to give the baby away. Wangeci denied having signed such papers, but Susan's words confirmed what she already suspected: Her baby was alive, probably in the home of the powerful politician in Washington or a member of the millionaire club.

"Betty told me you are going to help recover my baby," Wangeci finished, and looked straight at me.

Her mother, too. And Wainaina. And Mwihaki, who had come back in the room. I suppose Wangeci had agreed to meet me under that assumption. I felt tears, but I had to be strong for her, for the baby, for all the eyes on me.

"I will do all I can," I said. At the door, I turned. "Wangeci, I know it hurts. But please tell me the man's name."

She hesitated and started sobbing, then blurted out the name: Mark.

"Mark," I repeated. "Is he . . ." I couldn't find the words.

"Tall white man," she replied.

Shocked, I went over to sit on the floor near her and clasped her hands in mine. I held back my tears with difficulty. She sat on the floor, level with me, and hugged me. I could feel her heartbeat.

Afterward Wainaina would tell me that the sight of two black women in sorrow and solidarity would remain in his memory forever, that he so badly wanted to take that picture but couldn't bring himself to break the stillness. The whole world was absorbed in the silence of our embrace.

I stood up, feeling weak from what I now knew, or thought I did, about Mark's intimate involvement in adoption agencies. The dream of a landscaping business empire in Africa was a metaphor of a reality remembered. He was talking about the past and not the future.

"Hold my hand," I whispered to Wainaina.

I was sure he could feel me tremble.

19

Maina was fast asleep. He wiped his face with the back of his hand, adjusted his seat, then started the car, blaming the slumber on his allergies. The road was deserted except for a blue Toyota Land Cruiser parked a few hundred meters from Wangeci's house. I could not get my mind off Mark. I reflected on his put-on ignorance of Africa and Wangeci's testimony.

Down the road a bit, a vehicle hit us from behind. It seemed to come out of nowhere. I was jerked forward. They rammed us again. I was thrown forward, but my seat belt steadied me. Wainaina crashed into the dashboard. "Damn carjackers!" Maina shouted as he accelerated.

A shot rang out. I screamed and covered my head with my arms. For a few seconds everything seemed to be moving in slow motion. Another burst of gunfire shattered the back window. I ducked behind the seat as shards of glass fell on me. I thought I had been shot. My mouth dried up. I closed my eyes. My stomach tightened into a knot. I tried to say something, anything, to sound brave, but another gunshot held me silent. I shook with fear and my legs were cramping.

Maina sped toward Ngecha into a potholed section of the Limuru-Tigoni highway. If the gun-wielding goons didn't, these potholes would surely send us to our death. The road was virtually empty of traffic. We had no one to help us or bear witness to our execution.

I heard another loud bang. I curled up more. Then I felt a soft warm trickle of something on my neck. I felt for it with my right. It was blood. "I've been hit! I've been hit!" I shouted.

"Keep your head down," Maina shouted as he hit a huge pothole that sent the car airborne. I heard a groan from Wainaina. "Dammit!" Maina cried. "Should we let these jackers take the car?"

"This is not a carjack!" Wainaina shouted, mirroring my thoughts completely. "Just drive!"

The engine roared without gaining us any distance from the pursuing Toyota. Maina swerved the car left, right, any way, at times driving two wheels on the road and the other two on the side, trying to avoid the potholes.

"Come on, come on!" Maina shouted, talking to the car. "There's a police station at Kiambu Inn. Just hold on! Almost there, almost there!" I hoped the car was listening.

There was a lull and then a loud bang. I felt as if I had been split into two. The Land Cruiser had pitched us into a tailspin, and Maina was desperately trying to regain control. Then came the unmistakable smell of burning rubber.

"It's the tires," Maina screamed. "Everybody stay put!"

After ramming us, the Land Cruiser sped past. Down the road, the driver did a three-point turn. The Land Cruiser was now facing us.

Maina started revving the car, more and more, without moving. I raised my head: His eyes were fixed in front of him; the sweat on his neck and his heavy breathing belied his bravado. I saw him wipe his forehead with his forearm. He shifted a little in his seat and then engaged the first gear.

"What are you doing?" shouted Wainaina.

Maina did not answer. Suddenly, he released the clutch and the car lurched forward, pushing me back against the seat. This is a bad move, I thought. Us against the Land Cruiser. It had started coming at us. I watched as, at break-neck speed, we closed the distance to our fate. This was suicide by car! I saw the man with the gun attempt to take aim and then duck inside.

I held my breath, closed my eyes, and waited for the inevitable head-on collision. Nothing happened. I opened my eyes and looked back in time to see the Land Cruiser swerve, lose control, veer off the road, and disappear down the cliff. We just heard the impact as we sped down and then up the Kiambu hill all the way to the police station.

Maina explained his suicidal gamble. Hired gangs are motivated by greed, not ideals. The dead don't collect money. His plan B was to swerve just before the collision, but the assassins blinked first. We gratefully recorded our statements at the police precinct, confining them to the chase. Luckily, no one was badly hurt. I had just suffered a cut on my left hand. We left the battered car at the precinct and took a bus.

On arrival at Jane's place, I called Wangeci to brief her on what had happened. I did not want to scare her, but I stressed that the Land Cruiser had been parked outside their house; that obviously the men knew we were there and were waiting for us to come out. Wangeci told me that they had heard the gunfire. She promised she would be careful in her movements.

Alone, I went over the recent sequence of events. Ben. Wakitabu. Supa Duka. Father Brian. The photo. I recalled the surveillance video back in the Bronx and the car chase that followed it. Now here, so soon after a surveillance photo—though an old one—we had survived another car chase. Both came after my contact with Ben. Father Brian had come into the mix, complicating the way out of the maze. Was there a connection between Ben and Brian?

A call from Wainaina confirmed the limitation of time. Betty had sent him an urgent message: Wakitabu was looking for me. I was being hunted from all sides. I had to find a way out of the maze. Once again I had to go back to the beginning: the Alternative Clinics and its founder, Sister Paulina.

20

The next morning found Jane and me driving furiously to our old school, Loreto Convent Msongari in Lavington. I had not been back since I left, and despite being weighed down by the events, I was curious about the changes. The bougainvillea-lined road leading to the school entrance was intact. The fishpond had been replaced by a rose garden. But the group of nuns walking in single file across the compound toward the chapel brought fond memories of my four years at the school.

"Power, remember her?" Jane asked.

"How could I forget. I was terrified of her."

Power was the nickname we had given to Sister Ann, our headmistress, who exuded and exercised power. And no one, not even Jane the daredevil, wanted to cross her path intentionally.

Jane parked opposite the chapel a few yards from the statue of Mary, mother of Jesus. We had always wondered what became of the chocolate birthday cakes we left at her feet. Were we not on a different mission, it would have been fun to ask one of the sisters.

We walked past the music rooms. I peeped in. The pianos were intact. As we entered the staff room, we were greeted by a short, plumpish woman in a blue habit and a deep blue dress over a light blue blouse.

"Sister Paulina, good to see you again," Jane said as they hugged. "This is Mugure, also a former Msongari student. Mugure, Sister Paulina."

Sister Paulina led us through to the dining room. The tables looked smaller, as did the chairs, telling me I had added a few inches to my height since those days. We sat at a table near the door. She offered us tea and chocolate cake. I supposed there was no need to ask about the fate of the cakes meant for Mary.

After a few pleasantries, Jane delved right into the reason for our visit. "Mugure has just come from the States. She is doing fieldwork on teen HIV, sex, and pregnancy. To that effect, she has been living in Kambera. But why don't you tell Sister what you want?" she said to me.

"Thank you for agreeing to meet with us," I said. "I have come across too many cases of teenagers and young mothers getting pregnant routinely. I met one young woman who gets pregnant three months after delivery. I was told of others who carry twins, triplets, even octuplets. There's a common theme: They have been to or are connected with clinics and adoption agencies that mushroomed after the ban on your Alternative Clinics. And they are silent about the babies. I believe the roots of the problem, the mystery, are to be found in the closure of Alternative Clinics."

"Sister Paulina," Jane chipped in, "I believe that the Alternative Clinics were fine, clean, with absolute integrity in their operations. They offered immaculate services, if I might put it that way."

"That's why we are here. To see if you can answer a few questions," I said.

She listened intently, her eyes on us all the time, but with no reaction. Now she said, "It depends on what you want to know. I haven't followed up on all the things that have happened since our closure."

"Why do you think they let you go?" I asked.

"I was the leader. I am not aware of any other reason," she said humbly but obviously choosing her words carefully.

"Sister, if I might say so, those who wanted you out had ulterior motives," Jane said.

"I did my part. I still believe we were doing the right thing."

"Why do you think the Church came out so aggressively? It's not as if the state had a strong case against the Alternative Clinics—that is, if they had one," I persisted.

"I really don't know. But yes, they were a bit rough," she said, and laughed as she stirred sugar into her tea.

"Why do you think the Alternative Clinics were banned?" I asked her directly.

"I don't know," she said.

"Do you think Alternative Clinics may have been doing something that could be construed as out of the ordinary?" I tried again.

"Not to my knowledge," she said, shaking her head. "As far as I was concerned, we were helping those girls. I don't believe in abortion myself, never have, so I couldn't possibly have condoned that, you know?"

"I know, Sister, I know. The way Father Brian came out blazing, it's like he knew something." Jane said.

"Why do you think Father Brian testified against the clinics?" I asked.

"It's very hard to know people's hearts. Only God knows."

There was nothing for us to say after that. We hadn't learned anything new. The conversation had simply raised more questions. As we stood to leave, I said, "Sister, I understand that you had an audience with the pope at the Vatican?"

"Yes, but it's not a matter I can discuss."

"He must have talked to you about the secret document, asked you questions, given you a fair hearing?"

For the first time, I saw something cross her face, a slight movement of her brows. Her lips trembled a little. I don't know but I believe she was holding back tears. Then she composed herself. "I cannot talk about it."

"Sister, I believe the clue lies in that document. And Father Brian is at the center of it. I have personal reasons to believe that Father Brian may be an evil presence. Anything you can tell us about him, your observation, your gut feeling, little things, might help save lives."

I noted that she did not deny or confirm or even say, as she had done with the questions about the Vatican, that it was a matter she could not discuss with us.

"It was really nice having you here," she said to Jane. "Thank you for all you did, God will reward you. And thank you for bringing the visitor."

She led us to the door. Jane was very quiet. Her failure to protect the Alternative Clinics still weighed heavily on her, and meeting with Sister Paulina had clearly awakened the pain. For me, Sister Paulina came across as a genuine person who had tried her best to be honest without maligning anybody with a turn of phrase or tone of voice. But she could not mask her pain. She stood at the door as if undecided whether to follow us or go back inside. Then she called us back. "The document contains a vision of evil. Only it was not our vision. Please find the document and stop the evil, if it has not already started." She went back in the house as if weakened by the weight of her statement.

Jane and I drove most of the way back in silence. Jane broke the quiet when we arrived outside her gate. "I suppose the Vatican had to let her go. What with all the scandals involving priests in America, Europe, everywhere, pedophiles even, the Vatican could not afford another scandal."

We found Wainaina at Jane's house and briefed him.

"What made you ask her about the document?" Jane asked.

"You. It figured strongly in your story. Remember the picture that Brian gave me?"

I told them about the suited gunman back in the States and his demands that Zack give up the original document. Zack had spoken as if it were just one among many legal documents. But the document that the gunman demanded from Zack referred to a particular one signed at Shamrock. What was the connection between Zack, Brian, and the document? As far as I knew, Zack first set foot in Kenya on our honeymoon, which was confined to Mombasa. And except for numerous phone calls that could come from anywhere, Zack had depended on me.

It seemed to me that the document, whatever it contained, linked many people who were seemingly unconnected, at least judging by the few facts that we knew.

"We know that Susan, a Protestant, and Brian, a Roman Catholic, set up their agencies or clinics after the collapse of the Alternative Clinics. Were they coordinated acts, or did they emerge spontaneously out of the ashes? We now know that Alaska is ALASKA. It is also the mysterious Kasla. Has Brian ever been to America? Yet he is connected to the gunman. And the car chases and Mark and Joe? I suspect they are all involved. But it's not enough for us to know that they are involved. We have to convince skeptics. Which means we have to connect the dots. We must trail Susan and Brian."

"I am with you all the way," Jane said with a smile. She could tell that I had made up my mind. It was as if she had seen her own daredevil in me.

21

"Not you guys again," said the security guard after he opened the gate for us. Wainaina and I had waited until dark before we made our way to Reverend Susan's offices at the Miracle Church. We had parked by the roadside, way outside the church's premises. Our previous monetary handouts paved the way, and Kamau admonished us more as old friends than uninvited callers. He had company, he told us.

We took him aside, a few feet from the gate, and told him in low conspiratorial voices that we wanted access to the office. At first he refused, gesturing toward the company—too dangerous, what would happen to him if something went wrong—but I suspected these were Kamau's negotiating tactics. We offered him some money. He said he would talk to his colleague. Even his friend wanted to eat. After a few minutes of haggling, we settled on a sum and paid him in dollars. "Just like the Americans!" he said, seemingly satisfied.

It turned out that he did not have the office keys, the rogue, but after a few more dollars—*baksheesh*, or tipping, as he called it—he offered to open the windows. "They are wide enough for an elephant to go through," Kamau said.

Wainaina was all for it. He was an intellectual who could talk Kant with professors and cut through any bull-shit or play dirty when necessary. We were happy to take the risk.

"Don't mess the office up," Kamau warned us, but it looked like he was enjoying his role in the conspiracy. He even lent us his flashlights so we wouldn't have to put on the lights.

"Don't do a Murdoch/*News of the World*," I said to Wainaina lightly as we jumped into the office.

"Perpetrate crime to generate news?" Wainaina said.

"You could be out of a job," I said, and we laughed nervously.

It turned out not to be an easy search. The table was cluttered with many papers and folders. Wainaina went straight to the filing cabinet. "Shit, it's locked," he said.

I tried the drawers next to the window. Scanning through quickly, I saw a brown folder and recalled Magda telling us about such a folder. I opened it and, with the flashlight, saw a list of names. "This is it," I whispered to Wainaina.

We pored over it. The first list had about a hundred women's names with an X or a Y next to each name. I assumed they were the owners of the wombs for hire. There was another list that, judging by the largely foreign names, contained the recipients of the babies produced under the contract. We knew Kamau would not let us pilfer it. "No problem," Wainaina said, pointing at the copy machine in the next room. Just then Kamau tapped the window. Our time was up.

"We will be right out," I said.

Wainaina was already making copies. After five minutes, the watchman shouted again. I promised him more money in exchange for another five minutes. Wainaina was almost done. I took the ten or so pages that he had not copied, and stuffed them in my bra and in the back of my jeans. Wainaina stuffed the rest inside his coat pocket.

"She is here . . . she is here," the security guard shouted.

"Who?" I asked.

"Reverend Susan. Get out, get out," he urged us frantically.

We heard a car honk. Wainaina and I rushed to the window. The file, the file, I remembered, rushed back, grabbed it, shoved it back where it had been, and followed Wainaina out the window into the flower bushes. The car's bright lights shone on us as she drove into the compound. I felt the bushes shaking but then realized it was me.

From where we hid, I couldn't see Reverend Susan clearly. But she had company. Three people. I heard footsteps. This was not good. Had the guards set us up? I held my breath as the footsteps came closer. They stopped by the window on the inside.

"You should always close these windows, Reverend, mosquitoes are plenty this time of year," a male voice said.

All I could do was nudge Wainaina. I had recognized the voice. It was Daktari of the Supa Duka.

"C'mon, honey, leave the windows alone," a woman called out to the doctor and chuckled. "We have a lot of work pending. I have lined up a few Hollywood stars. My singing tour has garnered me many clients, even in Rio. The demand for adoption is really very high." Then they entered the offices.

This couldn't be real. I felt light-headed. I couldn't breathe. I didn't know how long I stared, wide-eyed, trying but unable to say a word. Festival of Rags, yes, but this? Wainaina sensed something and put his arm around me. But how to tell him that the woman who spoke of beneficiaries of the wombs for sale was Melinda? Why, Melinda, why?

The watchman hovered over us and whispered, "Now." We followed him out; his companion walked us to our car.

Melinda's betrayal weighed heavily on my mind. Even when Wainaina gave me the loot from Susan's office and I retired to my room, I felt so drained that I did not have the energy to look at the papers. Instead, I shoved them under some others. I wanted to lie on the bed in the dark to wrestle with my thoughts. Melinda, Melinda. She was part of this network of evil.

I never wanted to see her again. But there was no way I was going to connect the dots by hiding from the fight. I had to take it to them. I knew I would have to confront Melinda. But where, when, how? Then I recalled she was due to perform at the Festival of Rags.

22

This year's Festival of Rags was being held at Manguo grounds, near Ngarariga, Susan's birthplace. Manguo used to be a marshland, a habitat for varieties of birds, animals, and plants. But a shoe factory, with the blessings of the colonial state, had turned the marshes into a dump site for the poisonous waste from the tanneries. The marshes became inhabitable to birds and other forms of animal life; even more, useless as a catchment. But the grounds were flat and extensive and, in the dry season, could hold a crowd of thousands.

We parked outside the fenced field, one of hundreds in the huge space assigned to cars. Jane, who had never attended the annual event because, like Magda, she thought it mocked the poor, had been reluctant, but a smooch from Wainaina accompanying his "please" clinched the deal. I believed she also had a sneaking admiration for Susan's will and ability to manipulate the male rules of the world.

Wainaina had brought a camera to take as many pictures as he could, but mostly of those around Susan. He was to secure a date to interview Melinda for the *Daily*

Star, a prelude to one with Susan. I put on a pair of jeans and a tattered T-shirt. Jane wore a nice dress and a woolen shawl with a beautiful pattern of holes. Soon we were lost in the milling crowd of tatters and masks of misery. White and Asian visitors wore black masks, mostly, but their hair or a bit of their faces might give away their race and color.

Inside the makeshift stadium, miracle vendors in rags sold sunglasses that could shield the wearer from a satanic gaze; bottles with holy water blessed by Reverend Susan; T-shirts with emblems of the holy tree under which Susan founded the Miracle Ministries; bags and badges with pictures of Susan basking in rays that came from Jesus. At the podium were five men guarding a tree decorated with a white ribbon and a red carpet around it, a replica of the original tree. The tree had healing powers, and for a few hundred shillings, members of the public were allowed to touch it. The queue was long. A few women dressed in white wings of rags walked around burning incense to drive away evil spirits that may have lodged themselves among the faithful.

Jane and I followed closely behind Wainaina till we settled on a spot that gave us a good view of the stage, under a huge tent. The band played gospel music. Next to the band but at a distance sat the ragged VIPs and dignitaries, among them members of Parliament and the business community. Reverend Susan's robes were silken. Maxwell Kaguta, the powerful minister of faith and religion, in golden African robes pinned with patches of rags, sat next to Susan. It was obvious that their rags had been designed for this occasion, a dramatic contrast to the ordinary folk who came in their daily clothes.

After the prayers, the master of ceremonies, dressed in a silk suit with patches stuck on, apologized because some of the notables had not arrived. But there was a special guest, the star of the day, and she would sing first. "Meet the woman with the voice of an angel," he said.

Melinda shot from someplace behind the tent. She was dressed in a flowing maxidress with little star shapes stuck to it. She was the Melinda of Shamrock, only now, with the sunshine and the massing crowd hushed, she looked even more dominant and powerful. Looking at her, so beautiful, I almost began to doubt she was the Melinda of the other night. She came charging, glory, glory, and soon everybody was raising their voices. *Mine eyes have seen the glory of the coming of the Lord,* she said, and then sang the chorus:

> *Glory, glory, hallelujah!*
> *Glory, glory, hallelujah!*
> *Glory, glory, hallelujah!*
> *His truth is marching on.*

She started with very low notes working to very high. Even I who had heard her so many times could only stare in wonder. Here was the preacher side of Melinda. From the chorus she would seamlessly recite: *I have seen him in the watch-fires of a hundred circling camps.* And then the chorus of glory: *I have read a fiery gospel writ in burnished rows of steel. Oh yes, glory, glory, hallelujah. In the beauty of the lilies Christ was born across the sea.* Glory, glory. She whipped the crowd into joining the chorus; it became a call-and-response. *He is coming like the glory of the morning on the wave,* she intoned. She was not done. "Glory," she called out, and the crowd returned, "Glory."

The crowd was hysterical. Then she introduced the Miracle anthem. She talked movingly of how black people were forced into slavery; she described the harsh conditions of plantation slavery; the whip lashes, the wounds. And that was how the spiritual was born. They looked to their future deliverance and sang:

> *Swing low, sweet chariot*
> *Coming for to carry me home*
> *Swing low, sweet chariot*
> *Coming for to carry me home*
> *I looked over Jordan, and what did I see*
> *Coming for to carry me home*
> *A band of angels coming after me,*
> *Coming for to carry me home.*

A wireless mike in hand, Melinda moved among the crowd as if singing to each and every individual in that gathering. By the time she came back to the stage, everybody was clapping and singing with her. A thunderous roar greeted her when she asked in song:

> *If you get there before I do,*
> *Coming for to carry me home*
> *Tell all my friends I'm coming too*
> *Coming for to carry me hooooooooooome.*

She was not faking it. She sang her heart out. Wainaina stood there, his camera frozen in his hands, glued to the flawless soulful performance. Jane was singing along. For a moment even I forgot the events of the night at the Miracle Church, thinking with regret, even pain, How could so many Melindas inhabit the same body? I missed this Melinda, the woman with the voice of an angel, the one whose voice blessed my first night out with Zack, the voice that sang for me at my wedding. Her preaching—the side I had not seen—told me why she and Susan had clicked; from all accounts, Susan, though she could not hold a note, had the power of the word.

And then the master of ceremonies called for silence. The expected guests had come. I had not seen their arrival because of the hysteria all around. Like Melinda before them, they emerged from behind the tent one at a time. I recognized the first guest immediately: Daktari of the Supa Duka, introduced as Dr. Peter Kunyiha. I had hardly recovered from the shock when the master of ceremonies announced another special guest from America: Miles Jackson Sanders. He was more than a name to me. He was the Rhino Man from the Manhattan curio shop. He was part of the Susan and Melinda entourage.

I motioned Jane and directed her to Wainaina to make sure he captured pictures of Daktari and Miles, any grouping that showed them together and singly. Jane moved and was soon lost in the crowd of rags.

Strange, I was thinking, that every time I thought I was about to connect the dots, others appeared to complicate the process. There was some progress: The Daktari and the Rhino Man had names, and I had been able to connect them to Susan. What about Father Brian? Could he be here, dressed in rags of the Catholic order?

Suddenly I felt something jab my ribs. It was a gun. The man wore a leopard mask and motioned me with jabs to walk to the side. Wakitabu, I thought, and froze with fear. A scream would have been lost in the noise, besides blowing my cover wide open. I walked slowly, as directed, trying to figure a way out. Sam's dad had said I should arm myself. I wished I had a gun of my own, but it was a wish born of despair. At the edges of the crowd, the man took off his mask, deliberately revealing his face and then masking it again. It was not Wakitabu.

It was the suited gunman.

"Tell me where he is hiding, and you're free."

"Who?" I asked, perplexed.

"Don't play games with me. Give us Zack."

"Zack is in Estonia," I said.

"He was there, all right. He vanished in Tallinn, the devil. I followed him in Latvia and lost him, but he can't escape me forever. Lead me to where he is hiding or—"

"He's in Estonia," I said firmly. "Not here. Not in Kenya. He does not even know that I am here. If you want to kill me, do so, but I have no information on Zack."

I heard the click of the gun. I closed my eyes and waited for the pain.

"What are you doing here? Eyes closed? You scared me," I heard Jane's voice beside me.

I opened my eyes. The gunman had gone. I held on to Jane, trembling, tears flowing. She asked, "What's the matter?" I did not have the voice or the strength to answer her but hoarsely said: "Didn't you see him? In a leopard mask?" Jane asked, "Who? Where?"

"Let's get the hell out of here," I said finally.

Melinda was singing again, and the crowd was going crazy, as we wound our way back to the car. Jane phoned Wainaina to join us. He was bubbling with excitement because he had managed to get Melinda's business card and an invitation to set up an interview. One look at me was enough to cool him down.

We drove in silence, and it was only when we were safe in Jane's house that I was able to tell them about the suited gunman. The noose around me was tightening. Just to check up on things, I called Zack. No answer. Dammit. Ben, no answer.

I swallowed my pride, my anger, my hurt, and decided to try the number Ben had texted me. I went to my room and dialed the Criminal Investigations Department. "May I speak to Detective Johnston?"

"Speaking," a deep voice boomed. "What can I do for you?"

"Hi, my name is Mugure. I got your number from Detective Ben—"

"I have been expecting your call," he interrupted. "I understand you have some information for me?"

"Yes, sir, but now it's urgent. My life is in danger. Where can we meet?"

"How about you come to my office?" he replied.

"I am not so sure that is a good idea. I believe I am being followed. Being seen coming to the CID headquarters may send a signal."

"Not a bad signal to send to a person with criminal intent, but shall we say the Serena Hotel?"

"Sir, come to the anti-corruption offices within the hour. Someone will meet you there and bring you to me."

He chuckled. So patronizing, I thought, but I was not about to take chances. Every time Ben contacted me, something bad followed. I had to keep in mind that Johnston was Ben's friend.

"Okay," he said, "I will play along. But the information better be useful."

I told Jane and Wainaina my fears, and we came up with a plan. Jane sent her secretary to meet Johnston at the anti-corruption offices and bring him to Room 54, booked under Jane's name.

My first thought when I saw the tall detective enter the room was that he was too lean and too bald to be in law enforcement. He wore a tennis shirt with a pair of blue jeans and white sneakers. "Oh, it's Wainaina. I am a fan," Johnston said as soon as he spotted him.

"Thanks," Wainaina replied.

"You," Jane exclaimed.

"What a small world, ha?" he said, stretching out his hand to her. "The last time we met, you wanted to strangle me."

I looked at them, wondering if they had been seeing each other. "Why?" I asked.

"Remember the case I was telling you about?" Jane said. "He was the detective fighting me. The guy who relied on a corrupt Catholic clergy to fight a virtuous Catholic clergy."

"If I recall, you are the ones who painted criminals to look like they were women's rights advocates. Man, you guys would do anything to win a court case," Detective Johnston said.

"But we did not rely on rumors and a secret document," Jane responded.

"The Vatican agreed with us. Father Brian was commended and your 'holy' sisters reprimanded."

"Whoa, cease fire," I said, sensing this might not end up well.

"I agree with that," Johnston said. "Look, Jane, the case is closed, so there's little point in talking about it."

"Okay, Detective Johnston, let's shake hands. A truce," she said.

Then she excused herself. She would be at home or in her office if we needed anything. She left with her secretary.

Wainaina and I sat on the bed and Detective Johnston on the chair next to the bed. A small world indeed, I thought. Ben's Johnston the "brave" was Jane's Detective "Mbaya."

I gave him a narrative of everything I'd learned since my return to Kenya. When I got to the part about in vitro fertilization, Detective Johnston could not hide his disbelief. "Some woman who has been fired from her job tells you she suspects that Reverend Susan is manufacturing babies, and you buy the story? Are you sure?"

"If you just let me finish," I said. I then told him about the women in Kambera and about my visit to the Supa Duka clinic in Mashingo.

"What?" he said in shock, then repeated, "Are you sure?"

Now I had his attention. "Look, I am not insane. Naive, maybe, but of sound mind and, I believe, some bit of intelligence."

"This is interesting. If it is true, you—we—have to be careful," he said, as if to himself. "Especially if Maxwell Kaguta is involved. He is well connected. He can make one disappear into thin air like that." He snapped his fingers. "Yes, we have to be careful."

His inclusive "we" was encouraging. I felt at ease. I poured my heart out. But the moment I mentioned Wakitabu and the suited gunman, he became skeptical. I held my ground. "Wakitabu is a police officer," I continued. "He terrorizes the women. And he is after me."

"Are you accusing the police force of being stalkers, murderers, and kidnappers?"

"Please, Detective Johnston, talk to him, at least. And while we are at it, can I please look at the document?"

"What document?"

"The one you and Jane were talking about. I believe it contains the solution to the mystery—a master plan for evil, as Sister Paulina described it."

"You talked to her? Then why did she not tell you its content?"

"Because she did not write it. And she's so full of integrity that she refused to impute any improper motives to you or Brian."

"Please, Mugure," he said, clearly trying to be as polite as possible but hardly able to disguise the fact that he had been touched by Paulina's refusal to assign blame. "Leave everything in our hands."

The gunman from the festival took his attention. He asked details of face and dress and mask and gait. He asked me to repeat the words spoken. He wore a serious countenance. "Tell you what: Should the gunman accost you again, please call me."

As a token of his serious intent, he gave me a code to his direct line. He stood up to leave, looked at me as if he had something else to tell me, changed his mind, and left.

"We are on our own, it seems, " I told Wainaina. "Do you know how I can get a gun?"

Wainaina was taken aback, but if he thought I was crazy, he did not show it. "I am afraid I know more about the pen than the gun," he said.

"Okay. Tell me, when and where is the interview with Melinda?"

23

The interview was going to take place at the International Hotel on Grand Street in the city center. Jane lent us her car. Armed with a camera and a flash, I posed as Wainaina's assistant. There was no answer from Melinda's room when we arrived, so we went to wait at the bar. We ordered mineral water. On our second attempt, she answered and invited Wainaina up to her penthouse suite.

Melinda was all smiles when Wainaina entered, and she apologized for being late. She had been to a meeting of the organizing committee for a possible international Festival of Rags, to be held in New York City. At first she did not recognize me, but when she did, she froze. Then she turned around and pulled the door to the sleeping chamber shut, presumably to give herself the time to get composed.

"Mugure, when did you . . . ? What a nice surprise." She smiled as she walked toward me, then stopped in her tracks. My face must have said it all. What I really wanted was to jump on her and pull the demons out myself. I remained calm, or rather, I tried.

I said, "That glory thing was wonderful. And the pane-gyric about slavery and the birth of the spiritual . . ."

"You heard me? Were you at the festival?"

"How could I miss it? So how many clients did you get in Rio?"

She offered us seats. Wainaina sat down on a sofa, but I remained standing.

"What are you talking about, Mugure?"

"Oh, you have forgotten so soon. I'm talking about babies snatched from their mothers. Cheap labor, slave labor, the poor made to produce for your clients in Rio and Hollywood?"

She seemed baffled. Then again, this was what she was good at.

"And Sanders. Miles. No wonder you took me there to confirm that Kasla was closed. Melinda, you really knew what you were doing, didn't you?"

She was silent, almost paralyzed; she did not try to deny or confirm, just stared at me with wide eyes. Did I detect fear? But I was not armed. I had not even threatened her. I went on, suppressing my anger with difficulty at the memory of the deception, the crocodile tears, the manufac-tured sympathy.

"And Mark, your Mark, breeds babies in Africa. How can you? You are back with him, I know. But how can you?"

This seemed to unfreeze the statue she had become. She came to life. "Listen, Mugure. Mark has never set foot in Africa. All those landscaping dreams were exactly that: pipe dreams. To impress you."

"You lie. You lie, preacher woman. Protecting Mark?" I said as I moved toward her, determined to make her talk.

I don't know what overcame me, but I started taking pictures of a frightened Melinda. She may have thought the camera click and flash were some sort of weapon, because she let out a scream and took a step back. But her eyes were looking past me. I turned around.

The suited gunman stood at the door, gun drawn. I had not heard him fling open the door. He pointed the gun at me as he took steps toward me. I thought he and Melinda had plotted this: They must have met at Shamrock. But when he got closer, he waved me to a corner, with a warning to Wainaina and me not to do anything silly: "You scream, you die." We hid behind the sofa. It was now Melinda and the gunman.

"Where's Zack?" he asked Melinda.

I didn't know what was more dumbfounding, his question or Melinda's hesitation. Was he confusing her with me?

"I count from one to five. At five, I will start shooting. Your leg will go first. Where's Zack?"

Melinda hesitated. Looked at me and then at the gunman.

"Don't you look at her. She doesn't know his whereabouts. She does not even know that her Zack knows Africa, Kenya, inside out. I expected him to be at the festival. But you, you do know where he is, you always know where he is, because you work together. And you are going to tell me," the gunman said, and started counting. "One, two, three . . ."

"I . . . He is . . ." she stammered in terror.

It was like something from a horror movie. The bedroom door was flung open. Zack came out, gun blazing. Caught by surprise, the man stood still for a second, then fell to the ground, his gun skidding over to where I was cowering. Zack didn't once glance at me as he dashed for the door, Melinda following. But he stopped briefly at the door, wagged a finger at me, and ran out. It was almost a replica of the gesture Mark had made when he threatened me over his divorce.

I did not know what to think or even whether it was not an illusion. Scales had fallen from my eyes, and I saw a Zack I had never set eyes upon. Wainana and I were alone with a dead man. I wanted to get up but continued to stare at the gun and the body. Wainaina stood up, urging me to do the same. Then I heard shuffling by the door. Murderer Zack coming back? I didn't wait to see. I snatched the gun from the floor, jumped to my feet, and trained it on the man at the door, standing in the same spot the suited gunman had. I could hear the voice of Sam's father urging me to aim, aim, aim, and shoot.

"Mugure?" Ben said in shock, with his gun trained on me.

"Don't think I won't shoot. Put the gun down, Ben Underwood," I said. "Where is Zack?" he asked as he put the gun on the floor.

"Your friends just left after killing him," I answered, motioning to the man on the floor.

"What . . . you think . . . Oh, c'mon, sister, listen to me. That man on the floor works for Brian. He is a crook, and so is Zack. David West—you remember him?—has been working for me. He told me everything he knows. That's why we let him out. I have been following the crook, but he has been elusive. I was patient. I knew he would make a false move. And he did: stopping you at the Festival of Rags. Yes, I was there. But I lost him, thanks to the traffic. I have been on their trail. Well, I have, and now Detective Johnston is. The longer you keep me here, the more time Zack has to plan his escape. I can call you later to explain. And I'll tell Johnston about him." He pointed at the dead man.

I lowered the gun, not because I fully trusted Ben but because I did not have the strength or the will to shoot anyone. I needed all my energy to digest what I'd just seen and heard. Ben dashed out. After Zack, I hoped.

Wainaina and I followed him out. I put the gun in my handbag. Things had happened so swiftly that I did not know what to think or feel. But I had to accept reality. Zack may have been a crook; now he was a killer on the loose with Ben and Johnston after him. I was surprisingly calm as Wainaina said over and over again: "My! You can handle a gun."

I went straight to my room, switched off the lights, and lay on the bed fully clothed, my mind clogged with thoughts of the unimaginable that had become a reality: Ben and the gunman at the Festival of Rags; Zack and Melinda in the same hotel in Kenya. Though I had seen it, I could hardly envision it. Other images competed for attention: Melinda and Zack had maintained a relationship throughout my marriage; Melinda was a liar, with all that stuff about Mark never setting foot in Africa, maybe carrying on with both Zack and Mark; Melinda, the blood angel, was a key player in Susan's adoption activities; and Zack was a murderer. Then there were Mark, Miles, Brian, and Joe. How did they all fit in the puzzle? Nothing was stable in my life anymore. No, no, I should not say that. There was Kobi. My thoughts turned to him. His life was going to be greatly affected; there was no way I would let a murderer back in his life. The whirling thoughts and images kept me awake, but finally, somehow, I must have fallen asleep.

The following morning, my body felt heavy, but I dragged myself out of bed. I felt weak. I had not eaten well the last few days. I thought a cup of coffee would perk me up. Then I saw my handbag: The weapon of the dead gunman was there.

Last night's events came back in all their clarity and hit me afresh. Where I had felt calm under pressure, now I felt my heart soften. I was trembling. I began to weep. Silently. My calm had been a self-protective façade. As hard as it was to accept what had happened, I had to get ahold of myself.

I called Ben. My feelings toward him were suspended between suspicion and gratitude. The pattern of good alternating with evil after every meeting or contact had followed me to Kenya. His appearance could be a setup.

"Ben, what happened after?" I asked after he picked up the phone.

"Sister, the time I took talking you out of shooting me gave him and Melinda a head start. I lost them completely."

"I am sorry," I said.

"I told you about white conspiracy. Rosie agrees—"

"Don't you even go there," I said. "I am slowly recovering from the shock of revelations."

"I am sorry, sister."

"Ben, I would have liked to welcome you better in Kenya than with the muzzle of a gun snatched from the hands of a man killed by my husband. Tell me, did Joe really think I was crazy?"

"Yes, when he first contacted me, but when I questioned him and his story did not add up, I got worried. I questioned him again, even threatened him. You know the rest. I must say, I am upset that you did not use the hotline."

"This needs a face-to-face," I said, returning his words to him. I can then read your body language, I thought. The case of Zack and Melinda had deepened my distrust of appearances. "I have a lot on my plate right now. Perhaps after I have more things figured out."

I remembered Wangeci, her mother, Betty, and all the other victims of wombs for hire. I was on a mission. I had more dots to connect. It was time to get back to work, despite the shambles that my personal life had become.

I remembered the papers that Wainaina and I had pilfered from Susan's place. I made some coffee, then sat at the dining table with all the papers spread out. There was the sheet with the names of women and X or Y and dollar figures. Then there was the list of foreign names. Recipients of the adopted children, I guessed. "Abducted" was a better description. Adopt, abduct, adoption, abduction. Next to the foreign names were acronyms of their home countries, covering Europe and North America.

Standing out on the "donor" list were some names crossed out in red, with "replaced" written next to them. I recalled my encounter with Kivete, the director of appearance. The Miracle Church was constantly being cleansed of people who might bad-mouth it. Cleaning. Cleansing. Could these be the women who had resisted giving up their babies? Or posed a threat to the nefarious goings-on? Oh, and Betty was going to resist. I had not been in touch with her. She had warned me against Wakitabu. I must get in touch with her. I dialed her number. No answer.

I continued to study the list. I stopped when I came to Wangeci's name. The X or Y next to her name had been crossed out. Why cross out the letters when her name was already crossed out? Was it because, as Betty had said, Wangeci was a special case? Wait. There was some faint writing at the top. I sat back in the chair and took a deep breath and then looked at it again. It was almost as if I feared to know. The name stared at me.

Kobi, my son, was Wangeci's son.

I stood up, holding the piece of paper. Then I sat down again. Though I closed my eyes, thoughts continued drumming. Kobi, my son: Wangeci's son. No wonder her niece had looked so familiar when we visited their home. She resembled Kobi. I felt relief that her son, my son, was alive and well and that I loved him. But that feeling came along with deep sadness, even panic. I had no right to him. I pulled out my wallet and looked at the picture of Kobi that I always carried. He looked like Wangeci. No, I had no right to him. But I loved him, even more so now that I knew I would have to protect him from Zack. What madness was this? Why was this happening to me? Had I done something wrong? My life had been rather stable, but everything had fallen apart. Did I deserve it? I felt like I was being punished for having sold my soul to a devil.

There had to be some other explanation. How was I going to deal with this? I would have to fight fate, if necessary. If I quietly slipped out of the country, I could keep my son. Wangeci had already lost him. For a moment I pictured a life of bliss for Kobi and me, away from Zack, away from anybody who might be in a position to know.

No, no. I banished those thoughts. It would never work. Conscience would never let me rest: Wangeci's appeal would haunt me forever. I had to do the right thing. I had no claims on him. I must reunite mother and child. I would show Wangeci the picture.

I could not handle it alone. Not with the events of yesterday coming back to me in a very different light. Dangling the piece of paper from my hands, I half ran to Jane's room and knocked. I knocked again, a little bit more insistently. Eventually, a sleepy Jane stood at the door, wrapped in a robe. Wainaina stepped up behind her.

"My son is Wangeci's son," I blurted.

"What son?" Jane asked.

"Kobi," I said, and looked at them.

"The boy who was taken away from her," Wainaina said, somewhere between a statement and a question.

"Give us a minute to get dressed," Jane said as she pushed her way back into the room. So I walked back to the kitchen to wait.

"This is not a matter that I can tell Wangeci on the phone," I told Jane and Wainaina as they entered the kitchen. "I must see her in person." They agreed.

When I called Wangeci, there was no answer. I called the landline. Her mother answered, crying. "Wangeci has been kidnapped. Help."

I did not have the words. "I'm coming now."

I called Ben. He and Detective Johnston came over to Jane's place. "Please help us rescue her," I said.

"You stay put," Detective Johnston said. "Ben and I will go there with my boys."

"Oh no, Detective," I said. "We are coming."

"These guys are dangerous. You stay here."

"Don't underestimate her," Ben intervened. "I know she can handle a weapon."

"It's true," Wainaina said.

Ben and Johnston looked at each other. Of course they had talked about what had happened at the hotel. In fact, Wainaina had told me that Johnston had called and begged him not to publish the story yet.

"You still got it?" Johnston asked.

I nodded.

"Let's get on with it."

Detective Johnston was at the wheel, Ben next to him. Wainaina and I sat in the back. Wainaina had printed the pictures he took at the Festival of Rags. I looked at them one by one. I leaned forward and handed a photo to Ben. "This was the man at the Manhattan curio shop."

"This explains his sudden disappearance from New York. He was coming to the Festival of Rags."

"And to get more curios from Susan." I explained the connection between Miwani of the sunglasses logo. "Ben, you pooh-poohed my attempts to link the two. Remember?"

"At this rate, sister, you'll soon take my job," Ben said, and laughed, and then told me that David West had confirmed the connection with Edward and Palmer, but he did not elaborate.

"There's a connection between Kasla and Alaska," I explained. "And Father Brian is the father—"

"Catholic priests don't marry," Ben interrupted.

The word "priest" brought back the memory of Brian and his threat. I told Ben about my encounter with the priest. "The priest who sent those messages," Ben said.

I took out the envelope with the picture and explained

that it had been taken outside Shamrock, the same scene I'd told Ben about at the airport. Ben became serious. "Sister, can I keep the envelope and the picture? I want to send it to our labs in America tonight," he said without explaining.

Of course it was okay. I was glad that I had not thrown it away. I called Wangeci again. As before, it rang without a response. I was about to hang up when a man's voice came on. "I was told by a friend that you were asking too many questions. You didn't stop. It looks like only death will stop you from asking questions." Click!

I must have looked like I had seen a ghost. It was the same voice that had threatened me on the phone back in the States. It was the voice of the Rhino Man, Miles Jackson Sanders. I briefed Detective Johnston. "Ben is aware of Miles. We have been looking at his picture, thanks to Wainaina," Johnston said.

Within a few minutes we were in Tigoni. We drove up the palm-lined road to the compound, but instead of the beauty I had seen on my first visit, I saw hiding places for thugs and murderers.

Detective Johnston's phone rang as we were getting out of the car, and he remained in the car to answer it. Ben stayed with him. Wangeci's mother was standing outside. I ran to her. She hugged me. We went inside the house, holding hands. Her eyes were red and swollen. Inside was a host of people I presumed were Wangeci's relatives and/ or friends. The mood was somber.

"Can we talk somewhere?" I asked her mother.

"Yes, let's walk outside," she said.

Wangeci had been snatched outside the gates of the house, she told me. She was about to get to the details when Ben and Johnston came over. I introduced them. Detective Johnston pulled me to the side, leaving Wangeci's mother watching us three confer.

"They have found her," he said. "They found her body at Tigoni Dam."

Everything stood still for a few seconds. I wanted to erase what I had just heard.

"Mugure, you have to let them know," Johnston said, almost in a whisper. "It's always best when someone in the family breaks the news. I will go to the dam and then the Tigoni police station, but I'll be back in a short while. Ben is coming with me. I need cover. Those bastards cannot be very far. We'll phone for dog service at Tigoni. Now, Mugure, listen to me: Do not, I repeat, do not leave this house without us." The two walked away. He reiterated the bit about not leaving the premises to Wainaina. And they were gone.

I turned toward Wangeci's mother. The look on my face must have spoken a million words. Before I could say anything, she retreated, shaking her head. "No, don't tell me . . . don't tell me. Don't say the words."

But I told her exactly what Johnston had just told me. She collapsed in a heap on the veranda. I let her cry. I sat next to a very quiet Wainaina on the couch near the entrance, giving her the space to weep alone.

Then a woman came out of nowhere and rushed toward me, grabbed me by the shoulders, and pushed me backward. I tried to regain my footing but tripped and slammed into the table full of drinks, then rolled over and hit a couch with my back. Wainaina was on his feet, restraining the woman, who was screaming at me, "It was you, you who got her killed. She had been quiet, but you, you made her talk, and now she's gone."

I could not speak. Two men got up and pulled her out of the room as she kicked and screamed obscenities at me. Another woman helped me up, apologizing. "I am sorry, she is just mourning. Wangeci is her cousin and best friend. You are doing the right thing, and I hope you get the bastards."

That didn't make me feel better. I felt guilty and confused. It was best if I removed my face from the scene. There was enough pain without my adding to it.

"I badly need some fresh air," I told Wainaina, who followed, cautioning me against going outside the compound, repeating Detective Johnston's warning. "Leave me alone," I said.

As soon as I was well out of view from the house, I started crying. I cried for Wangeci; I cried for the women in the house; I cried for the women who had been forced to sell their own flesh and blood; and I cried because I was not sure I could do much to help them.

By now I had reached the gate. I turned and saw Wainaina walking fast after me, at the same time dialing his cell phone, perhaps calling Ben and Johnston. Outside the gate, I started walking faster, faster, faster, though not sure where I was going. Everything seemed unreal. I could feel my body shutting down, as in the moments before you fall asleep. I tripped on a stone on the roadside. The shooting pain from my toe woke me from my delirious state. I looked back to see Wainaina frantically looking around. I stopped.

"Let's go back in and wait for the detective by the gate," Wainaina implored me.

The words were hardly out of his mouth when we saw a black SUV coming toward us at high speed. I started to run to the gate, but I felt as though stones had been attached to my feet. I dragged them along against the cold Tigoni wind. The SUV was gaining on me. Kobi's face flashed before me. I must not die. I felt a surge of adrenaline. My feet were not obeying me. I tried to stay focused on the gate, but I kept glancing at the oncoming car. It was here. I heard Sam's father's voice: Aim, aim. In a matter of seconds, I had pulled out the gun and held it firmly in my hands. Aim, aim, aim, Sam's father urged me. I shot at the SUV, shattering the windshield.

The SUV swerved and drove past. I aimed and fired again, trying to get one of the tires. It drove on.

My knees gave way. I felt Wainaina grab my hand and pull me forward, with such force that I almost fell. He dragged me along and did not let go till I collapsed in a trembling heap on the sidewalk inside the gates. Wainaina sat opposite with a bead of sweat rolling down his forehead. We sat like that until a honk at the gate announced Ben and Johnston's arrival. Wainaina told them about the shoot-out.

They didn't even get out of the vehicle but drove in the direction of the SUV. They came back after an hour to report that they had caught up with the assassins. The vehicle had rolled over on the side a quarter mile after I had fired the gun: Rhino Man, aka Jackson, had been at the wheel with a bullet in his forehead, they reported. They didn't know if he had an accomplice; they had handed over the case to Tigoni police.

"Let's go after Father Brian," I told the two detectives.

They looked at each other and then at me. "Take a rest. We can resume the hunt for Brian tomorrow," Johnston said.

Johnston dropped Wainaina and me at Jane's house, telling me again to "just rest. You've done plenty." They were going to work on all the leads. I thanked them. "Give me more bullets, I shot my gun empty," I said, and Ben did. But the way he looked at me told he was not sure that I would obey the order to stay put.

I turned to Jane and Wainaina. "Brian is the missing link, and we must get him to talk. He must know that something has happened to his gunman. If he hears through his criminal grapevine, he may vanish. We must get him by hook, crook, or gun. Today. Tonight."

24

Jane was behind the wheel, Wainaina in the passenger seat, and I was in the back. He talked ceaselessly about my way with guns. I had taken him by surprise first at the hotel and later, at Tigoni, when I hit a moving target. I could tell that Jane was anticipating the next phase of our quest: a kind of citizen's arrest of Father Brian.

Carts loaded with goods told us that we had reached the Donkey City. Wainaina jumped out of the car to ask for directions to Father Brian's church or house. Jane sat in the car. I took the opportunity to stretch my legs. Then I spotted a small open-air market selling bananas and oranges. I felt hungry. I was picking out the best bananas when a woman approached me.

"Are you one of them?" The contrast between her ragged clothes, torn in places, and the tote bag she was swinging was striking. "God sees you, He sees all of you," she said, and then walked away, laughing. A few steps down the road, she changed her gait to imitate the walk of a high-heeled lady, swinging her bag in rhythm. "Don't mind her, she has been like that for many years," said the woman selling fruit.

"What happened?" I asked.

"Her baby died. Born with a single kidney, they told her. They would not show her the body. She became depressed. Sometimes she will ask you to look in her bag for the baby sleeping in there."

Wainaina was already in the car when I got back. He and Jane pounced on the ripe bananas, and as we munched, I told them about my encounter with the woman. Some aspects of her story were similar to Wangeci's, I said. And the tote bag. I had seen similar bags with Wangeci, Philomena, and Betty. I remembered that I had not made the second call to Betty and immediately dialed the number. Again, there was no answer. I voiced my concern: Betty had told me she wanted to keep her baby. She had said she would run away but . . .

"Why don't you call Philomena?" Wainaina said,

I did. Philomena answered but did not let me edge in a word. She spoke in a whisper. "Please don't call again. They took her away last night."

When I tried to ask who "they" were, she hung up. I tried again, but she had switched off her phone.

"They have taken Betty," I said.

I called Detective Johnston. No answer.

We waited until the first cover of darkness and drove to Father Brian's church. An old white Datsun pickup was parked beside of the church. I got out of the car and gingerly approached it. There was no driver inside. I made out MCC, written on the driver's side. I guessed it referred to the Mashingo Catholic Church.

A line of toilets was built on the right side of the church.

I went back to our car. Jane suggested she remain in the car in case things turned sour. I took my bag and flung it over my shoulder. The gun was still there.

So Wainaina and I were on the hunt for Father Brian. The doors were locked. I peeked inside at the wooden benches on which were hymnbooks and Bibles. Father Brian was not around. But did I really expect to see him on his knees? I walked around the back.

At the far end, I could make out the outline of a wall. I walked slowly, prying in the darkness, Wainaina following close behind. The wall was too high for me to look over. I spotted a loose rock and dragged it closer to the wall and, standing on it, was able to see on the other side, where I beheld a house whose full size was partly obscured by trees. The entrance must have been on the other side. A pair of jeans, socks, and a tote bag hung on a line to dry, near a security light that dimly lit parts of the compound. The image of the woman and the tote bag flashed in my mind.

"Let's check out that house," I said, stepping off the stone.

"How?" Wainaina asked.

"We let ourselves in. The way we did at the Miracle Church. You and I have become experts at this kind of thing," I said, trying to lighten the atmosphere.

"Burglars who almost bungled it last time," he said.

Wainaina pushed me up, then jumped over easily. We were burglar, with Jane as the driver of the getaway vehicle.

We lay low under some bushes. A stench that hit my nostrils made me think of dog shit. Dogs! What if they had dogs? But why would they keep attack dogs in a church? It was quiet. A security guard walked across the compound, shining his flashlight here and there, and disappeared in the back. I felt for the barrel of the gun, more as an assurance than anything else. After what appeared to be a long time, the guard walked back and entered his little hut by the gate.

Minutes later, we crept up to a window and peered inside. The room was dimly lit under the door. We walked along the walls of the house past another window whose curtain was not drawn. We were just able to make out a bed and a wardrobe.

"We better leave. There's nothing here," Wainaina whispered.

"Yeah," I said, feeling a bit let down. Then I heard a cry. A baby's cry.

We moved toward the sound slowly, listening. It turned out to be a big house that went farther into the woods than we had assumed. We came up to another window and listened. This was it. The baby had stopped crying, but we could hear some movements. I looked in the window. This was a nursery. There were ten to fifteen babies asleep in little cribs. A woman was trying to pacify the crying baby with a bottle. She looked somewhat older, and as she rocked the baby, she closed her eyes. Just then another woman, much younger, came in and quickly checked the babies, woke the woman up, gave her a little verbal lashing, and then left. I recognized her as the nurse at the Supa Duka Clinic.

Wainaina stood next to me, and even though I didn't see his face, I could feel his outrage.

Babies packed in a warehouse, waiting to be shipped out: This was a police case. We must try Johnston again.

25

With Wainaina trailing behind and my armpits drenched in sweat, we tiptoed back to the wall. I struggled and then managed to grip it. Wainaina pushed me up onto a narrow landing on the wall. I was about to jump over when I turned for a last glimpse of the house. I saw a light coming from an obscure place among the trees at the far end of the house, the part adjacent to the church. We had not seen that light when we were peering into the baby warehouse. Someone must have just turned on the light, I thought. That window was lower than all the other ones. I jumped back down and tiptoed quickly toward the little window, about ten yards from the one where we had seen the babies, beckoning Wainaina to follow.

It was a basement window. This raised my curiosity a notch. Basements are an American phenomenon, the East Coast mainly, rare in Kenyan architecture. I bent down to take a peek. The window hadn't had a wash in a while. I pulled up my sweater sleeve, folded it around my palm, and tried to dust off the window. Then I pressed my face against the pane. All I could see were boxes.

"Can you see anything?" I whispered to Wainaina, who was scrunched over as well.

"Just boxes. Oh, and a fridge, I think," he said. "They look like kitchen appliances."

I looked around the yard, trying to figure out what to do next. I wanted to go inside, but I couldn't see a way in. Except through the window. "We have to break in."

"You're kidding, right?" Wainaina said.

"No," I said.

"There has to be another way," Wainaina said, feeling his way around the small window. He tugged at it until the little window creaked and then gave way. He was the first to jump in, and I followed. We huddled behind a huge cabinet that stood adjacent to some small filing cabinets. The musky, damp smell was unmistakably mildew. I was standing so close to Wainaina that I could feel the warmth of his breath and his chest going up and down. There was nothing here except the huge boxes we had seen from outside. Some kind of storage, I thought.

"Let's climb back up," whispered Wainaina, and I nodded in agreement. He added, "I will help you up first, but I need a chair."

Then, almost simultaneously, we saw a door. Maybe that was a better way out. Wainaina gently pushed it open, peeked through, and then walked in. I followed suit. We tiptoed along the corridor till we came to a very small room with a huge sink on the right and scrubs hanging on the wall on either side. Straight ahead was a swinging door. It seemed like a house of rooms within rooms; it reminded me of a Russian doll I once bought for Kobi. We pushed right through, and the door gave way to a huge tiled room. The big overhead lights were similar to the ones at the Supa Duka Clinic.

The windowless room appeared spotlessly clean. Three big clocks showing three different time zones, New York, London, and Tokyo, hung on the wall. They looked incongruous, creepy, an impression strengthened by the other items. A stainless-steel table dominated the middle of the room, a small table filled with surgical tools and a cart with huge cylinders right next to it. Below the table were trash bins lined with plastic paper. It was a clinic, yes, the same high quality as the Supa Duka, except that it looked less like a birthing place than a cross between a morgue and an operating theater.

On my left was yet another door. I tried the handle; it was locked. Walking away from it, I tripped over an empty carton and stumbled a little before finding my footing. Then I saw Wainaina standing still, his hand over his mouth. I quickly ran to him. He was staring at what resembled a cooler with small connecting tubes jutting out, a see-through cover, and a thermometer by the side. I bent to take a closer look at some plastic bags.

Staring back at me were what appeared to be human body parts. I picked one bag and peered into it. Baby kidneys, arms, body parts.

I felt an intense mixture of pain, anger, nausea, fear, and repugnance, followed by shooting pains in my stomach. I felt like throwing up. I thought of all the women, Betty, Grace, and Philomena: the mothers.

I must not throw up. We have to leave, I told myself.

We heard the shuffling of feet coming from somewhere

behind us. I saw another door to my left. Without thinking, I pulled Wainaina by the hand and made a quick run
for it, pulling the door closed behind us. Except for a strip
of light under the door, we were in total darkness. The
light under the door went off. We heard nothing. I assumed
that the man had left it on by mistake and come back to
rectify his error. Now the room was completely dark. We
waited for a while. The silence was deafening. Wainaina
felt about on the wall for a switch, I guessed. Sure enough,
light flooded the room.

I saw a short flight of spiral stairs and went for it. At
the last step leading to a door, I came to a small window
and saw Jane's car parked in the yard. I realized abruptly
that the church stood on the body parts laboratory. The
door was locked. Break the window, or yank it open like
we had done with the first? I looked behind me to ask
Wainaina.

"Wainaina?" I whispered, but he didn't answer. I
walked back down. "Hey, Wainaina?"

I felt a sharp pain in my head. Dizzy, I turned around
and saw a male figure looming over me. I knew too late
that my gun was still in my bag, hanging from my shoulder. I kicked hard, aiming at his balls, and heard him grunt.
Then silence and darkness.

I must have blacked out, for when I awoke, I was alone
in a room. I tried to move but found that my hands were
tied. My head was throbbing with a pain that shot to my
temples every time I tried to move. I looked to the side
and saw Wainaina slumped down and tied to a chair. A
thin trickle of blood from his mouth dripped on the floor.
I could hear his faint breath, so I knew he was alive. I tried
to move my legs, and they felt numb; I realized they were

tied, too. "Wainaina, Wainaina!" I hissed, but he didn't respond.

I heard footsteps and a mumble of voices. The footsteps became louder. Enter a slightly limping Wakitabu, and with him a no longer pregnant Betty, strapped to a wheelchair. Was the crying baby in the nursery warehouse Betty's? I wondered. She had a lost look on her face, like someone who had been drugged. I felt so powerless, I hated myself. How could I have forgotten to take the gun from the shoulder bag? I made as if to move toward her.

A slap across the face sent me on the floor with the chair. I attempted to get up, but I couldn't. Lying on my side, I saw Wakitabu move over to Wainaina and shake him into consciousness. Then he came back to me and lifted me, still tied to the chair, from the floor.

"I want you and you," he said, pointing the gun at Betty and Wainaina, "to see what I'll do to this woman." He pointed the gun at me. "I will teach you to hit a man's balls. I will teach you not to interfere in matters that don't concern you. Fake Amina. You played with my mind, ruined my otherwise spotless record at Kambera. I will break your legs, your hands, one by one, a slow death." Though he was shouting, he was grimacing with pain. There was not a hint of mercy on his brutal face. We were all going to die.

From somewhere inside, I gathered whatever strength I had and expressed my contempt. "Do you also eat the babies you help slaughter? The women you help murder?"

"You . . . You . . ." he said, fuming with anger, pointing his gun at my left leg, while Wainaina and Betty begged, "Don't."

He took his time, trying to exert maximum terror. I closed my eyes. I heard a familiar voice.

"Go easy on her."

I opened my eyes only to see Wakitabu hop to the side meekly. My savior stood at the door. I was torn between hurrah and horror.

It was Zack with a gun in his hand.

26

Zack led me to an adjoining room and pushed me into a chair. The place was bare, but it could have functioned as an office. My bag dangled from my neck. I did not want to draw undue attention to it, but I hoped my gun was in there.

"You betrayed me to the gunman? You were together, weren't you? Maybe you were always together from the beginning. I should have let Wakitabu finish you off. With that journalist. Arranging an interview . . ."

They were not the words I had expected to come out of his mouth first. His narrow escape from death at the hands of the man who had hunted him across countries and continents had left him more bitter than grateful. He stood behind the desk, gun in hand, piercing me with his steely gaze. My disgust and contempt for him would not let me dignify his allegations with silence.

"I was not with him. He thought I knew where you were. He must have followed me. I would not get any satisfaction from your death by hands other than mine.

I would like to strangle you and squeeze every ounce of breath from you."

Zack burst out laughing. Even I saw the ridiculous side to my wish. My tiny hands squeezing that neck?

"Is that so? Now let's talk serious business between man and wife. How would you like this to end?"

I had no illusions. He would not let us go free. We knew too much. Our only ally was time. I had to keep Zack talking, give us a chance to find a way to the gun or for fate to intervene.

"So all those years were a lie?" I asked, surprisingly calm, more of a loud thought than a question.

"I have never lied to you. And no, I didn't marry you because of this business, although it didn't hurt that my wife was Kenyan. It was destiny, you know, when I bumped into you at O&O. When you bent down to pick the flying pages and then raised your head . . . Well, what can I say? You were beautiful. But I saw something else: You acted as if you were more to blame than I was for the bump. I needed that self-effacement in my life. Then you grew on me. My heart felt calmer, just knowing I was coming home to you."

"After stealing babies, Zack? Really?"

He started pacing. Keep calm, I told myself, thinking about my gun. Keep him busy with questions. Make him talk, talk, talk. He loves stories about himself.

"Those kids are living in the best homes all over the world." He paused. "As for the women, I rent their wombs."

"You rob them, enslave them, their body, their souls, and you call it rent?"

His laughter sounded evil. I wondered how I ever could have found it attractive.

"I didn't touch their souls," he said as he moved to the other side of the table and slumped into a chair. "I left their bodies intact. I paid good money."

"And got paid even better? You're killing babies? Why, Zack, why?"

He stood and walked a step or two away from the table, then turned to me. "Don't you see that we save lives? Stem cell research. Hundreds have been saved; thousands more will be. These kids have already saved presidents, prime ministers, Hollywood stars, priests."

"What? But their lives. Do they matter to you?"

"Restoring. Incarnation, if you don't like restoration."

"Just how many babies, Zack?"

"Not even close to those who die of starvation, disease, and the endless ethnic wars on this godforsaken continent. Your politicians, your government, they kill far more, and then play victim and kill more. I help these women. In exchange, they donate a little tissue to help save lives."

"Poor people's babies are mere tissue?"

He rose and sat down again. "You remind me of my father, who, unable to face reality, retreated into the *bottle field*. But my grandfather accepted that the weak feed the strong; the lower feed the higher. Wealth thrives on poverty. I didn't make up that part. It's the way the world works. Your Africa has been donating tissue to the West for centuries. Your politicians get a cut, that's all. I am not doing anything different. I am just a middleman."

"How did you get Melinda into this?" I asked. "Your lover?"

He seemed amused by the question. He was enjoying his own performance. "She loved me. I didn't love her. The more indifference I showed her, the more devoted she became. She would do anything for me. How do you think we got the reverend? When I met Susan in Estonia, I saw that her fantasies could be turned into profit. The Black Angel clinched the deal. It was easy. Melinda had the same savior fantasies. Where they saw salvation, I saw a way to save myself."

My eyes felt like they were burning, but I couldn't cry. I was shaky. I could have sworn the room was spinning; I wished Wainaina were near me to steady me. I have to handle this, I thought, even as I saw that I was standing still. I looked hard at Zack. I closed my eyes for a second or two, and when I opened them, it was still Zack standing in front of me. Who was this man, really?

"And their role? Susan and Melinda? Just fishers of poor women and children?" I was trying with difficulty to suppress my sarcasm.

"Melinda and Susan bring the women to have the babies and attend to them. The nursery. A full-time mother to feed them. Nurses to look after them."

"You mean the babies in the warehouse?"

"Yes. Some go for adoptions through Susan and Melinda. The others—"

"You act as God, deciding who will live or die?" I interrupted, wondering how he could talk as if describing an everyday occurrence.

"You don't understand. They all live. Some are adopted as part of a human family; others are adapted as part of a human body," he said. He stood and started pacing.

The man was sick, his words sickening. I moved my hand slowly and felt my bag. The gun was there. Zack, self-absorbed, was looking away from me. I figured out how to quickly open the bag and reach for the gun. Neither he nor Wakitabu, who was guarding Wainaina and Betty, seemed to suspect I possessed one. Wakitabu had not bothered to search me. Buy time, I thought.

"Did Melinda and Susan know about what happens to the babies who are not adopted? Who are for what you call adaption to the body?"

"What do you think? In our kind of business, we survive by making sure that the left is left and the right is right and never the twain shall meet. Women are too sentimental; let them take care of milk. Men take care of blood."

"By 'men,' you mean you, Joe . . ."

"Joe? Who in his right mind would involve a playboy like Joe in serious business? He's always thinking of how he can get a woman to bed."

Did I hear right? I had to make sure. "Why did he want to kill me?"

The question provoked prolonged maniacal laughter. "I don't know. At first I laughed. Then I realized that the video I had Melinda hand-deliver to our place had worked in ways I had not imagined. You thought she had already left for Rio. She knew you were taking me to the airport. I thought the chase would temper your curiosity, but I guess I was wrong."

I felt foolish and guilty about the risks I had taken that night, running away from a phantom of my own imagination. But what about Joe's conversation about calming me? Who was he talking to? Mark, maybe? "But you were willing to place your 'right mind' in Mark's service. Or you do you think that Melinda's denial deceived me? Why would you work for Mark while sleeping with his wife?"

"Ex-wife," he interrupted me. "Mark and his dreams of a global landscaping paradise, spiced with smuggling illegal immigrants? Too greedy. Too risky. Mark has never been in Africa. But he did help by keeping Melinda away from me, providing a cover, sort of, until their divorce."

"What about Kobi? Doesn't it bother you?"

"That he is my son?" he retorted.

"He is Wangeci's," I said.

"And mine," he said.

"I met Wangeci before you killed her. She told me everything about her and Mark. Mark made you adopt his child: Melinda's doing? Then he ordered you to murder children. You are nothing but Mark's attack dog."

At first he seemed confused, unable to get what I was talking about. Then he burst into laughter. "I see. I told you, you don't know what you think you know. My Estonian Finnish connections. Markus, my birth name—which is also my father's name—is a variation of the English Mark. You, as my wife, should have known that I use it for my other businesses. Call them aliases. For my work here, my alias is Mark, the English version of Markus. Wangeci knew me as Mark."

My knees were weakening. I recalled Melinda observing how Kobi resembled Zack. On reflection, I could see it for myself. It was his triumph over me.

"And Melinda? Did she know?" I asked weakly, almost seeking more time to digest what I had just heard: that Zack, as Mark, had fathered Kobi.

"Not about Wangeci and Kobi."

"Your own flesh and blood? You would have sold your son?"

"At the time, in my mind he was not, you know. You saved him. Your need for a baby saved him. And now I love that boy dearly. I cannot imagine life without him. I thank you for that. Where is he?"

"You had the mother of your child murdered," I said, avoiding the question.

"That fool Miles Jackson did it. Tell him to scare somebody, he scares the person to death. He almost did you in at the Starbucks in the Bronx. He was a bubbling idiot, mixed up the adoption papers, and I'm not surprised the police got him in the end. I don't kill people I have loved."

"So all that talk of loving me is just talk?"

"Why?"

"You're going to kill me. Do you realize that by killing me, you'll deprive Kobi of his remaining mother the way you were deprived of a father? Is that your revenge on history?"

"I did just fine growing up without a father."

"I see. So you found the father you lost in Father Brian?" I said sarcastically.

"Father Brian? He thinks he's smart. I drew a vision. It's in the document. I showed him the way, and he ran with it. He has acting abilities, that I grant. He turned the Vatican into a believer. A big achievement, in my humble view. But he had no idea what would be born out of the ashes of the Alternative Clinics. True, he registered the name ALASKA, but that was my idea. He enjoyed his new role, with the whole nation, from cabinet ministers to women and children, as the admiring audience . . . For him, the document had achieved its purpose. I could never figure out why he clamored for the original. For me, the document lives. Its purposes and vision have yet to be fully realized. Your curiosity almost ruined me. Your tricks—bringing those people to fumigate my office— you just missed it, didn't you see it when you rummaged through my library? The original document, the one that clearly outlines the vision of the glory of the future, was in the file marked 'Alaska.' You took a piece from it because of a telephone number and the name Kobi. Your curiosity almost tore down my vision for a domination that has eluded the strongest of men. I will not give you a second chance to destroy what I have already built. But maybe, just maybe, we can negotiate something if you tell me where Kobi is. If you don't fully cooperate, you know the end. After I'm done with you, it will be the turn of Father—"

"I am here, Zack," Father Brian said. "And don't turn around. Your wife can confirm that I am not a phantom. Fling that gun away. Do it." Zack obeyed. "Good. And by the way, Wakitabu is my man, not yours, Zack. He just called me about you. You killed my gunman and took away his gun."

Father Brian, still in his fake uniform of a Catholic priest, emerged from a door behind Zack. He stood slightly to one side, the rosary around his neck falling on his white frock, occasionally prodding Zack with the gun he held.

"Father Brian," Zack was saying in a tremulous voice, "I have been faithful in ensuring that your pay is intact. Edward and Palmer, my legal firm, has done well as a laundering center, providing legal defenses, and protecting channels. We have bribed customs and immigration officials from here to America. I have built a global network. The relations I have been trying to establish with Okigbo and Okigbo might bear fruit, and Nigeria will be the new theater of our operation. Look, Brian, I have always protected you, even tried to make my snooper of a wife believe you were an innocent bystander. And now you turn against me?"

Okigbo and Okigbo? I hoped not, but everything was unfolding, like a film noir, before my very eyes.

"Zack, you are a bad actor. When we first met at Shamrock, I mistook you for a reliable crook, like me. Now here you are, claiming the document as your sole creation? You're a legal mind. You know the name of what you're doing? Theft of intellectual property. I registered Alaska Enterprises as our umbrella company, and you say it's all your work? Your wife has more guts than you. As for the money, we agreed on equal shares, but you took advantage of the fact that I could not leave my adopted post of priest. You ignored all my messages and, in the end, killed the messenger, jeopardizing our enterprise. Wakitabu tipped me. You treat him with contempt: no respect for all the cleaning he has done for you. Now I cannot take any chances, so I need you to tell me: Where's the gun of my gunman?"

"I have it, Brian," I said, pointing the gun at him. "I tested it on Miles, but if you want proof that I can shoot, just resist. Put the gun down. Zack, don't move."

"So you are going to protect Zack?" Brian said laughingly, as if he did not believe me.

"No, I am protecting women and children from two monsters named Brian and Zack. I came here to get both of you."

As Brian turned around, I heard Sam's father urging me to aim and shoot. I made a Krav Maga move with my leg, and the gun flew from Brian's hand. As he rushed to recover it, I shot his leg. He fell on his knees. I saw Zack opening the door. I shot at him and missed. I shot Brian in the other leg, to ensure his complete immobility. I stood by the wall with both guns in my hands. When Wakitabu came toward me, shooting, I rained bullets from both guns. He slumped to the floor. I ran to the other room and tried to untie Wainaina. Though wounded, he had the strength to collect himself and help me free Betty. She had looked beaten and about to give up, but she seemed to acquire new strength. We handcuffed the uncomprehending Brian to the dead Wakitabu, back-to-back.

I said, "Wainaina, take a gun and watch the door. Betty, keep guard over this unholy monster."

Betty's reaction was one of disbelief and relief. "I want my baby," she told Brian, "or I will drown you with my piss."

I ran down the stairs, both guns drawn. I had to be careful because Zack could be hiding in any of the corners. But from a window, I saw a car drive past the gate. Zack had gotten away. I ran outside. Jane was on the phone in the car. I managed to reach Ben as soon as I was inside Jane's car, and I told him his man was waiting for him in the church.

"And Zack?" Ben asked.

"He got away."

"Mugure, we're coming. With reinforcements. Please stay put."

"Yes, Ben the African," I said. Jane got off the phone. "Let's go," I told Jane.

"What the hell is going on? I heard gunshots. I called Johnston," she said.

"Brian is saying the rosary on the floor. That's good, but right now, we need to go after Zack."

27

As we drove out to the Nakuru Naivasha Highway toward Nairobi, we were blinded by spotlights and deafened by the sirens of police cars. I was sure they were going to the house we had just left. But we didn't stop. I briefed Jane as she drove. She was speechless with fury by the time I finished. "You should have shot Brian dead. I would have done it."

"You're a defense lawyer, not a law enforcement officer," I reminded her.

We drove straight to Memories. I left Jane and went inside, where Kivete sat. I asked him to come back outside with me. "First a beer," he said, smiling, showing off.

I pulled out the gun. "Let's move," I said amid screams and shouts in the bar.

"Hey, I'm coming, I'm coming. Go easy," he said as he walked out with me and got into the car.

I explained to him as we drove away from Memories that it was time for him to help clean up the mess he had been party to. I briefed him on the baby murders. He was quiet for a moment, then told us that before he could do anything, we must first take him to Magda's in Kaloleni and ask no questions. I knew it was a risk we had to take.

We parked on the road and let him walk to Magda's alone. What a difference from the first time we had visited Magda! I would forever be grateful to her. Without her, we never would have known the story of Wangeci and Reverend Susan's register of stolen babies.

Then Kivete came back with her, got in the car, and asked us to drive to the home of Magda's friend, in the next neighborhood. Magda greeted us like old friends, but it was clear she looked at us with awe, admiration, and a sense of a comradeship.

At the friend's house, the two left the car. It was all a mystery. Five minutes later, Kivete emerged, cigarette in hand, with a sack bag slung over his shoulder. As he got in the car, he threw the cigarette butt on the ground and stepped on it. He did it with such force and determination that I knew this was not Kivete Kitete who danced at Memories.

"I have waited so long for this day. I have to atone," he said with a laugh, explaining that Magda had stayed at her friend's place.

"No, I am coming with you," Magda said, running toward us. She echoed Kivete's words. "I must be there when we confront Susan. Besides, I may be of some help. I know some things."

I said, "I want to know all about the secret meeting places, if any. When you were doing the cleaning, where did it take place?"

"Drive to the compound of the Miracle Church," he said.

I heard some noise that sounded like two metallic pipes clanking against each other, and turned back. Kivete had unloaded the little sack, and lying on the seat were two double-barreled shotguns. He looked up and saw me staring. "You know you can't go there unarmed. One thing I know about these people is that they will kill you to protect themselves," he said as he fixed the magazines.

I looked at Jane. "Maybe you should take one of these."

"I suppose I could," she replied, though unsure of herself. "Just in case!"

"I will stay with her," volunteered Magda. "All that training may be of some use."

We had come close to the gate. Jane pulled to the side. Kivete and I got out and walked toward the gate. I knocked. Kamau was getting used to seeing me. I waited for him to come outside, as he usually did. When he did, he said, "Today is not good. They are all in there. She has Americans. Besides, it's so late, why don't you come tomorrow?"

"I have to get in there," I said, brandishing some money.

This time he refused. "Really, they are all there, and I am under strict instructions—"

"Open the gate, Kamau," said Kivete, waving a gun at him. "Come on, my friend, you know not to waste my time." I was so afraid Kivete would pull the trigger. "Take the money and walk away," he continued. "Get yourself to Memories and buy a few beers. By the time you are done drinking, we will be done here!"

Kamau did not hesitate. He took the money I had brandished, got his small bag, and walked away. He didn't look back.

"Aren't you afraid he'll call Susan or the police?" I asked Kivete.

"Trust me, he wouldn't. He is going to Memories as we speak. He knows not to mess with me. Afterward, he will have a perfect story: Strange demons possessed him. If angels can fly the blessed from America to here, I am sure evil demons can fly an otherwise faithful servant to a bar against his will."

With that, we walked through the gates toward the church. I saw the car Zack had driven in the driveway, and two other cars, which I presumed belonged to Susan and her accomplices. We avoided the security lights, walking in the shadows. Kivete was walking in front of me, gun at the ready. I had mine as well. Then he started to run, half bent over, and I followed suit. We stopped in front of a small gate. This must be the gate Magda mentioned, I thought. There was a huge padlock on it.

"We need to jump," Kivete said.

Scaling walls and fences was what I had been doing lately. I tucked the gun in my jeans pocket and stepped on Kivete's outstretched hands. He shoved me up as I pulled myself up. I pulled my right foot onto the top and then, using my hands as an anchor, jumped. Kivete was soon beside me. We walked beside the walls, away from the glaring security lights. We walked until we got to the end of the building. I heard voices.

"Are you ready?" Kivete asked me in a whisper. I guessed he did not waste time. We had to do what had to be done. No need to dillydally.

Gun in hand, he tried the handle. Surprisingly, it gave way, and he stormed in with me right behind him.

Susan tried to reach for something in her bag.

"I am sure you know Kivete will not hesitate, but don't underestimate me, either," I said.

"Who are you?" Reverend Susan asked.

"Amina," replied Dr. Kunyiha, who was seated next to Melinda.

"No, this is my wife," said Zack, trying to look at ease, though I knew he was terrified. "I am sure we can talk about this as grown-ups. Brian was the bad guy, and you were right to shoot him. Who is this gentleman?" Zack asked, looking at Kivete.

"The guy who has been doing your dirty work, but not anymore," Kivete replied

"I was just briefing everyone here on what a shot you are, Mugure!" Zack said.

"C'mon, Mugure," Melinda said, making as if to come to me, as if we were nothing but old friends. What nerve!

"Don't, Melinda. Not now, not ever. Killing babies? Do you know Zack butchers babies, he and Father Brian? Body parts for export."

"We don't kill babies," Melinda said.

"We give them to parents with needs," Susan added.

"Zack set you up from the beginning. It's all in a document he and Father Brian drew up. Simple: You and Susan deal with milk. Men with blood . . . Tell them, Zack, tell them about the blood," I said, pointing the gun at him.

"Get on your knees," Kivete ordered. "All of you."

Reverend Susan was the first to fall on her knees. She said nothing. Dr. Kunyiha was next, and then Melinda and Zack, almost at the same time.

"What is she talking about, Zack?" Susan asked rather firmly.

"Oh, now you believe the woman with a gun to your head," Zack said.

"Stop your theatrics, we just want to know if there's some truth to it," shouted Melinda.

Everything after that happened in a blur. Zack dove forward, pushing Dr. Kunyiha to the floor. Kivete's shot caught Daktari in the shoulder. Zack dashed through the open door. I took aim but missed. For the second time, I had missed Zack. I ran after him into the inner room. It was quiet.

"Zack, you coward," I said, hoping to get him out of his hiding place. "You hide behind women's skirts."

I heard some sounds, and before I could shoot, I saw Zack run out of the room. I ran after him. I couldn't see properly in the dark and caught only glimpses of his shadow. He was running toward his car. Then it hit me: He must have a weapon in the car. My goal now was to get him before he got the gun. Then bright lights shone on Zack. Jane had turned her high beams on him. He paused. I shot at his car. He fumbled for his keys. I shot again.

I walked up to Zack. He knew he was cornered. He knew as well as I did that I would shoot him should he open the car door.

He turned around. "If you kill me, Mugure, you will never see Kobi again."

"You don't know that. I signed a pact with Wangeci."

"Shooting an unarmed man, Mugure? Now, now, now."

"I brought a lawyer with me. And a sharpshooter. If I miss, she won't," I said, referring to Magda. I was a couple of feet from him with the gun pointing at his head. Suddenly, I heard sirens and saw flashing lights, and I lost my concentration. Zack seized the opportunity and jumped toward me. I started shooting and kept shooting. He fell on me, sending me to the ground, blood spattering all over me, everywhere.

"Sister, sister," I heard Ben whisper as he helped me up.

28

I don't know why, but as I prepared to see my father, the words of Saint Paulina kept coming back to me: "It's difficult to know what goes on in the heart of a man." The questions persisted: Who was Brian? How could he have deceived everybody all the way to the Vatican?

It turned out, as I learned from Ben at a gathering in Jane's house—with Ben, Johnston, Betty, Philomena, Grace, and Magda—that Brian's real name was Stanley William. He had so many aliases that even this was not certain. He was a computer crook who worked for anyone who would hire him and was on the FBI's most-wanted list.

The real Father Brian was a God-fearing soul from Brazil, who on his very first visit to New York, happened to be at the World Trade Center on 9/11. He'd been planning to relocate to Kenya. Stanley William stole his identity, his name, his history, and vanished from New York.

Even Ben, with all his police experience, was baffled by the coincidence of two crooks with the most aliases working together. The question was, did they even know each other? Ironically, they met at Shamrock, Zack the master brain and Brian the master doer and actor.

"Brian works covertly, Zack overtly," explained Ben. "Brian stays in one spot and knows the environment; Zack travels under different aliases in Zimbabwe, Finland, Sweden, all over Eastern Europe. Brian is a crook who enjoys deception like one enjoys a work of art. Zack is driven by a warped view of the world and has neo-Nazi connections. Palmer and Edwards was a legal umbrella for many other enterprises, including Alaska, under which there were other, minor operations. He tried to lure Okigbo and Okigbo into the scheme, but Okgibo reported his advances to us. David helped us connect the dots in exchange for indemnity."

The document that he and Brian had drawn up was a manifesto and a vision of horror. It envisioned orphanage plantations to harvest human organs; human cloning factories in Africa, Asia, Latin America, and Eastern Europe, all clothed in the idea of a universal good. What had been going on in Kenya was just the beginning.

"And, Mugure," Johnston broke in, "I looked at the document again—at your insistence, I must say. All the horror stared at me afresh. Brian's evil genius lay in projecting the vision to Paulina and her Alternative Clinics. You might say it saves us from a moral dilemma."

"But why were they fighting for the original document?" I asked, still baffled.

"Ego," Ben explained. "Pretty much the way children fight over things. 'I got it first' type of thing."

I asked how the moral dilemma was solved for those who had escaped the judgment of the gun. Ben said that Brian would be extradited to the US. Melinda and Reverend Susan were arrested that very night. Susan was released at the insistence of Maxwell Kaguta, the minister of faith and religion, who claimed that she was an innocent victim of foreign mega-televangelists envious of her success. A victim of racism. Melinda was declared a persona non grata and somehow got herself on a flight back to the States.

"Interesting that both crooks clothed their evil with morality and legality," said Ben.

His comment reminded me of the debate between Wainaina and the philosopher at NYU years back about a universal ethical imperative. Was there an inner imperative that made humans clothe evil with holiness, or was it the universality of the simple statement that the road to hell is paved with good intentions? And yet for every Zack or Brian or Susan, there is a Sister Paulina, a Wainaina, a Jane, or a Betty who has learned to fight evil in their ways. I would like to cling to those moments, short-lived at times, longer at others, when good seems triumphant over evil. For me and, I suspect, the others, that moment was the reunion of Betty with her child. It was only appropriate that mother and child were the center around which the celebration at Jane's house revolved.

Questions remained, so many, but mostly about me—why I could not see what was in front of me. How could I have been so wrong in some of my judgments: Mark, for one. Melinda had painted him as the devil. His temporary disappearance was a visit to Mexico. He had never visited Kenya, and the suggestion of the Kasla agency had come from Melinda, its director, alongside the Rhino Man.

Joe was another. I had called him the previous night to offer my apologies. His late business call to some of his genuine business associates had sent me into paranoia. In speaking about calming her, he'd been referring to a client who was threatening hell because her mortgage had not come through in time. Joe had the good heart to play down how he had felt. He laughed at the absurdity of the chase: his complete puzzlement at my speeding up every time his car approached mine; and how his every gesture of peace was met with murderous rebuff. All would be forgiven, he said, if . . . But he knew my answer, he said, laughing again and thanking me for apprising him of the situation. "Oh, my friend Zack," he said, sighing.

I thought of Joe still describing Zack as his friend. Did he mean it? Who was I to judge history and others' actions in absolutes of evil and good? I had gotten Kobi through a crime committed by another. I had enjoyed money gained from unspeakable crimes. My education had been paid for, all the way from primary to university, by a father who would not see me and whose only moral instruction was for me not to fall into the hands of white boys. Melinda was black. Sam was white. Sam's dad, as conservative as they came, had taught me to defend myself. I had to admit that life is not always black or white, and when we get to read the blurred lines in between, life takes on another meaning.

I decided not to seek my father. I no longer wanted to confront him. I had Kobi to live for; he needed me now more than ever. My only problem was how I would explain to him the absence of a father in a manner that would satisfy without attendant trauma; and without creating a need to undertake endless missions about his roots or identify with a father seen through the romantic vision of loss and distance.

I did feel the need to visit my mother's grave before undertaking the one journey and the one encounter I dreaded most but which I knew I had to face: Wangeci's mother, now Kobi's grandmother. My mother, even in her grave, would give me the support I most needed. The certainty was founded on reason. Every time I visited my mother's grave, I felt a calm. *Gikuyu* people think of death as sleep, and for them, spirits mean the sleeping ones, *ngoma*, spirits. It gave me comfort to think of my mother as sleeping in peace but somehow able to hear me. These last few weeks, I had thought of her spirit as the mystery gardener who would not leave her precious herbs unattended.

It was a shock, almost—really, a disappointment—when I found the gardener in the flesh. I stood at the gate looking at him. I did not feel like communing with my mother in the presence of a stranger. But he sensed me watching him, and he walked over. "Yes, miss?"

"Oh, I was just admiring the garden, the herbs. Have you been working here for a long time?"

"No, no," he said, "the owner used to do it himself. He would come in his car, work on it, and then leave. Now he can't, so he gives me the flowers, or rather, he sends the driver to give me the flowers to lay on the gravesite. Diabetes is horrible. Not all the money GG had could save him from getting his leg amputated."

I had more questions but didn't ask. Complicated, really complicated. It was best that I leave. I just could not take any more. George Gata. The gardener was my father. I walked away without another word.

• • •

My next stop was Tigoni. It was important that I tell Wangeci's grandmother in my own words that the criminals had been arrested. I was surprised to find the small walk-in gate open. I wondered if I should ring the doorbell anyway. Just then I saw Wangeci's mother coming toward the gate. She was soon joined by Mwihaki and another woman I assumed was Mwihaki's mother. They came close to the gate before veering away. They were taking a stroll in the yard.

Why complicate their lives further? I didn't even know how I would tell her that the person who had ruined her daughter's life and eventually taken it away was also my husband, and that I was the beneficiary of Wangeci's loss.

Slowly, I turned my back to the gate and walked to the car. I told the taxi driver to stop by Tigoni Dam, where Wangeci's body had been dumped. I stood there, staring at the waters; my lips were trembling. I emerged from the dam a little stronger, a little calmer, clinging to the image of our last embrace. I wished that Wainaina had taken that picture. But did it matter?

Wangeci and I were forever joined by ties of motherhood to Kobi, whom we both loved.

29

The next day I flew to the US and went straight back to Sam's house in Ohio to reunite with Kobi and Rosie, as well as thank Sam and his father. Kobi and I ran toward each other. We embraced tightly, tightly. He seemed to have grown. Sam and Rosie were holding hands, with huge grins. I guessed Ohio was a romantic place after all. I called Mark who kept repeating, "I don't believe this," as I explained how his name had been misused. I felt I owed that to him now that Zack was dead.

I was still in Ohio when I received a text from Jane: She and Wainaina were expecting . . .

Acknowledgments

Many thanks to my literary agent, Gloria Loomis, for taking on the novel, and for making the business of getting published a smooth one. To Malaika Adero of Atria Books, a big thank-you for believing in the novel. I am really grateful to Henry Chakava for his creative suggestions; thanks to maitu Njeeri wa Ngũgĩ for detailed comments on the early draft; my father, Ngũgĩ wa Thiong'o, for the creative writing discussions/lessons and for being a fierce critic of the characters; to Sami Sallinen for the loving support and for poring over several drafts of the novel; to the children, Alem and Nyambura; to my siblings and fellow writers Tee, Kimunya, Ngina, Nducu, Mukoma, Njoki, Bjorn, Mumbi, and Thiong'o for reading drafts of the novel, sometimes twice, sometimes more, but most especially for the "nuggets"; to my nieces and nephews Nyambura (N2), Nyambura (N3), Biko, Miring'u, Chris, and June; to my friend Dorina Owindi for being there during the process of writing; to my friend Peter Kuria and the HAFF family; to my great friends Amkelwa Mbekeni and Liz Ndegwa for keeping it real—lots of love and light!

About the Author

Wanjikũ wa Ngũgĩ is a writer and director of the Helsinki African Film Festival (HAFF) in Finland. She is also a member of the editorial board of *Matatu: Journal for African Literature and Culture and Society*, and was a columnist for the Finnish development magazine *Maailman Kuvalehti,* writing about political and cultural issues. She has also been a jury member of the CinemAfrica Film Festival, Sweden, in 2012–2013. Her work has been published in the *Herald* (Zimbabwe), the *Daily Nation* and *Business Daily, Pambazuka News*, and *Chimurenga*, among others.

Printed in the United States
By Bookmasters